I0577443

First Edition, 2025

Cover Design: K. L. Thorne
Cover Images: Jupiterimages (Canva), Sergey Niven's (Getty Images), senoynoy (Canva), kanokthungchokechanchaicons (Canva)

Published by Niteowl Enterprises

Welcome, Reader

Welcome in, lovers of romantasy!

I hope you enjoy reading this story as much as I enjoyed writing it. With every draft, I fell more in love with Bryce and Ellie and I hope they find a special place in your heart and on your bookshelf.

Before we start, I want to warn you that this is a work of fiction. No person, animal or shifter were harmed in the research or writing of this novel. However, there are several potentially triggering aspects. To name a few:

Anatomy changes and descriptions during shifts.
Damaged vehicles.
Dangerous situations.
Kidnapping/held against their will
Weapons including knives and guns.
Violence, including descriptions of gore and blood.
Death by MMC.
Strong sexual content, including knotting and descriptive nudity.

Your mental health matters, if at any time you are unable to proceed with reading, please set it aside and prioritize yourself.

If you decide to read on, there is an accompanying playlist available:

- *"Animals" by Maroon 5*
- *"Let It Go" by Chandler Leighton with Lo Spirit*
- *"Hide and Seek" by Klergy and Mindy Jones*
- *"Paranoia" by Nathan Wagner*
- *"Middle of the Night" by Loveless*
- *"Wolf Totem" by The Hu and Jacoby Shaddix*
- *"Traitor" by Daughtry*
- *"God's Gonna Cut You Down" by Johnny Cash*
"Uncomfortably Numb" by Arrows in Action with Taylor Acorn
- *"Blvck" by Bryce Savage*
- *"Gym Class" by Lil Peep*
- *"Shake The Ground" by SNAILS, Kill The Noise, Sullivan King and Jonah Kay*

Enjoy!

For my truth, my Alethea. Thank you for loving me when I wasn't lovable, for being my best friend. To greatness! To glory!

Warning: This ebook contains adult language, steamy scenes, and growly male shifters. Reader discretion is advised

Chapter One

Bryce

"She's cute," Arick motioned toward the brunette at the bar that's been eyeing me, and not discreetly. I noticed her when we came in. Sarah? Susie? I couldn't remember her name. I looked around the dimly lit bar, watching a few guys play pool in the far corner. The bar was quiet, which is what Arick had wanted. It was just another late afternoon at the Maple Point bar. It was a small town our wolf pack territory had and all the locals knew each other. Some knew others all too well. I didn't bother looking back. "She thinks so, too." I offered, leaning back in my chair and eyeing my drink. I didn't really want it and only took a few swigs, but Arick needed to blow off steam. I motioned to him with my chin. "You should take her up on her offer. I'm sure she's lonely." I had an inkling she was, anyway. I hadn't talked to her in a month and didn't care to again. Arick messed up his face as he leaned on the table. "Too much on my mind." He released a sigh. "I don't know that I'm ready to be a dad to a teenager."

I laughed then. "A teenage wolf, at that. But Megan's a good kid, you'll be fine."

"Two weeks with my little girl, then she's almost a woman." Arick said, stroking the side of his glass bottle with his thumb. I sat quietly looking at my cousin, only older by a few days. The dim light of the bar didn't hide the wariness in his eyes. The lines near his eyes normally from laughter were now from worry. He still wore his leather riding jacket, he hadn't bothered to take it off when we got to the establishment and even with that and being hunched over the table, he was still recognizable as the Alpha. His tattooed hands cradled the brown bottle in his hands as he undoubtedly began facing the harsh reality his little girl was growing up. Wolves usually began shifting on the first full moon after their 12th birthday. It was then marked with a large celebration of the pack, and Arick took every opportunity to celebrate his only child. I believe partially to make up for her mother not being around. As I eyed Arick now, I knew he had been through a lot, too. He'd lost his mate when she had their first cub, and then he had been tasked with the difficult task of learning how to be an Alpha, a single dad and then burying his best friend.

"It's going to be an epic celebration," I said easily now, breaking our silence.

After running a hand through his sandy blonde hair, moving it off the collar of his jacket, he met my gaze and smiled, almost sad. "Yeah. I just wish Sarah could have seen how she's grown up."

I clapped him on the back. "She would be proud of the job you've done." I said as I stood. It was still light out, and I had some pack business to handle for the Alpha. And this conversation was getting too emotional. Arick and I worked together really well as long as we kept our feelings out of shit.

Arick nodded again. "Heard about Ellie? She's coming home." Arick explained before gulping down the rest of his beer. At the mention of Ellie, the air left my lungs and I had to sit down. Thoughts of Ellie had crept into my mind a few times in the last few years. Did she think about me? I would wonder, but then I couldn't help but think about her brother Tanner. As an orphan of the pack, friends are hard to come by, and Tanner and Arick were my best friends. The 3 of us had been larger than life until the night it all came crashing down. It was the night before Arick turned 21, when he would be named the new alpha of the pack. He had already said that Tanner and I would be his Betas, his second in command. Alphas were passed down by blood lines, but Betas didn't always mate and have an heir, so they were chosen by the new alpha. The fact that I had lost my parents and grew up on my uncle's charity and Arick still wanted me as his beta wasn't lost on me. Even though he was my older cousin, normally betas were chosen as people with intact families. The night before Arick took the pack we had all taken our bikes out, one last ride as a trio free from responsibilities. Then a car jumped the median and hit Tanner head on. Left to grieve him was his dad, the pack doctor and his little sister Ellie. She had been just fourteen at the time, just a kid. And she had worshipped the three of us as her brothers. I could still see the look in her eyes at his funeral. Like Arick and I had failed. We were heroes to her and we should have been able to keep her brother safe at all costs. But I had to face the fact we weren't immortal and grieve the man I had called brother.

After Arick had become alpha, Ellie had moved to the city to live with an aunt married to a neighboring pack. I shook my head and almost laughed as I downed more beer. Ellie had been just a kid, skinny and small. Her blond hair was always a mess and in a half-assed ponytail, her long arms hadn't quite caught up with the rest of her and her glasses had been too big for her face. Her freckles had consumed her face and I had always felt protective of her. Hell, all three of us had been protective of her. But losing one of her heroes was enough to break her and she had moved to finish school. Arick kept up with her through the Doctor, but I hadn't bothered. Because if I was being completely honest with myself, I agreed with her. I had failed Tanner. Ten years had passed, and I still didn't feel like it wasn't my fault. It was my idea for a moonlight ride and that put his death at my feet.

Grabbing my helmet, I shook my head to appear unphased. "I hadn't heard she was coming back. I'll see you at the pack house." The Alphas and Betas and their families all lived at the main pack house. Arick nodded and stayed where he was. "I'll be along in a while." Was all he said.

I walked outside and put my helmet on to protect my eyes from the bright September sun. There was already a chill in the air with October in just a few weeks, which made it the perfect weather to ride. As I climbed on my bike, I heard another one like my own approach. Always eager to check out machinery, I started mine and looked down the road and waited. Over the hill, I saw an all-black CBR come charging toward where I was, the rider wearing an all-black leather jacket, black jeans and black boots. I felt a frown crease my brow. I knew all the riders in our pack, this wasn't someone I was familiar with. As they approached with their head low to get under the wind, I couldn't help but see the outline of their body on the bike. It was obviously female, judging by the curvy ass I saw. Still getting closer, I saw the leather jacket did little to hide the large breasts that touched the tank of the bike.

A need I'm not sure I'm ready to identify took over my actions and before I knew it, I was putting my own bike in gear to find out who this person was. The bike zoomed past and I was already in motion. I had to know who this was. Rationally thinking, this could be someone from another pack here to start trouble. It could be a threat. In the back of my mind, I felt something more primal. Something I not only wasn't ready to name yet, but I wasn't sure I could. It was a force I hadn't felt before. A compulsion and I couldn't examine it at any length right now. Not until I knew this rider's identity. I was closing in and the closer I got, the nicer that ass looked. I saw a flash of my hands on it, holding it while the person it belonged to moaned my name. I shook off the thought and tried to focus just in time for a sharp corner in the road to take us. I couldn't help but notice the rider was extremely skilled and leaned appropriately to keep control of the bike. So it was someone who had been here before and knew the roads. This didn't bode well for my sense of security. Once we were through the turn, the rider in front of me saw me in her mirror and glanced over her shoulder. I gave a nod to acknowledge she saw me. To which her response was to give me a small solute and drop gears on the bike. The gap between our tires became larger and even matching her movements, I had more weight on my bike and she took off and down the road and I couldn't keep up. She took advantage of the gap and made a sharp turn to the right and even as I hoped that I could still see her on a country highway like we were on, once I turned the corner and began the path where she had gone, I lost all sight of her. I pulled over and nearly punched my bike. "Fuck!" Killing the engine, I pulled my cell out and dialed the pack house.

"Mr. Bryce, sir." Chad, the head of security answered the phone.

I didn't mince polite words, simply to the point because I was so pissed. "Let the border dogs know that we have a newcomer on a bike in the area. If they see anything, they're to contact me immediately." I couldn't stress the word enough. Chad disconnected the call and I knew it wouldn't be long before I knew where this bitch was. If she was trying to start trouble, she picked the wrong pack.

Ellie

I sat in the room that had been mine for the first fourteen years of my life. The walls were still deep purple, the molding around the top still black with glitter and black stars littered the white ceiling with soft white lights strung in between. The black yarn rug was still where I left it on my right in front of the door. The floating white shelves still had the books I read over and over as an adolescent. But my eyes stopped wandering as they landed on the picture in the gold frame. It was me and my dad on either side of my brother behind his motorcycle. My chest tightened as I remembered the day this was taken. I was so excited for him getting his dream bike I couldn't stop smiling, my braces bright in the sunlight. My light blonde hair up in a ponytail and the T-shirt and jeans hid my changing body perfectly.

My brother's arm was around my shoulder. His sandy blonde hair brushing the collar of the leather jacket my dad had gotten him to congratulate him on getting his bike. Dad's hair had just started turning gray at the temples, his broad shoulders were the same height as my brother's in his flannel shirt. Dad's beefy hand was resting on Tanner's shoulder, the other propped on his hip. His smile shone with his pride like only a dad's could. If I had known Tanner would be gone a year later, I would have begged him not to get the bike, not to go riding after dark. Not go riding with them. They were a tight trio, Tanner and his best friends, Arick and Bryce. I went to the desk in the corner and opened the top drawer where a similar photo was stashed away in a notebook. Only it was Tanner and his friends behind the bike. As I held the photo, I let emotions wash over me. Ones that I had pushed down for ten long years. Bryce had always been my crush, but I had been just a kid to him and Arick. Someone to be protected like a sister. I could still hear Bryce and Tanner cussing at Arick for taking me for a ride on his own bike. Arick had waved them off, unconcerned. He was the Alpha's son. Ten feet tall and bulletproof. Nothing would happen to anyone in his care. He was right as far as I had been concerned. I loved the wind rushing around my shoulders, tugging at my helmet. I had felt alive, free.

It had opened a new door for me that I hadn't recognized at the time. It would be the start of the path I came to know and love. After Tanner's . . . accident, I had gone to live with my aunt in the city. I couldn't be in this house alone with dad, not hearing Tanner come in at all hours of the night after helping Arick with hunts and watches. Not hear the shower running down the hallway, not hear Tanner laughing into his phone. The void that losing Tanner had created had been too much. Aunt Tess had been a haven, letting me switch schools and just be the quiet one in the corner. Away from all the sympathetic stares from the kids I knew in Maple Point. They didn't know me or my pain and I was happy with that. And then in my senior year, I met Matt. He showed me things about being a woman with a secret, how to work on engines for cash and I fell into a life and a path I was comfortable with. My dad had talked to Arick as they were always tight and Arick had said the pack mechanic had retired. In all his wisdom, my dad knew that might bring me back. If I had a place I could call my own to work on engines, cars and bikes without having to watch over my shoulder for the next set of scum bringing something in for modifications. Matt had been good at running off dead beats, but there was always someone with a score to settle. My dad had turned the garage under the house into a real mechanic's dream with two bays and lifts so I could work on pack vehicles as needed. The vehicles could have gone to the city, but there were always neighboring packs that could mess with vehicles and put the pack at risk. It was safer to have them worked on by someone loyal to the pack.

Dad had even said he'd had Tanner's bike brought home. I could work on restoring it, if I wanted. It sat in a far corner of the garage under a brown tarp. I hadn't been able to bring myself to look at it yet. I wasn't ready to face the reality of what Tanner's last few moments in this realm had been like.

The shrill ring of the phone beside my bed pulled me out of my thoughts. Dad insisted on keeping a landline as the pack doctor. I knew he was out visiting pack homes, so I walked across the room and picked it up.

"Hello?" I answered, still holding the picture in my hand.

There was silence on the other end, and I waited two breaths before continuing. "Anyone there?" But there was a shortness to my breath, almost like I was hoping to hear a familiar voice.

"Ellie?" It finally came and all the breath left my lungs and I felt my eyes close as the voice washed over me and pulled a million emotions to me, each one punching me in the gut. I wasn't ready, wasn't prepared for the weakness in my knees, ready to remember the last time he had said my name at Tanner's funeral. "I'm sorry, Ellie." He had said, reaching out slightly for me before dropping his hand to his side. I didn't have the strength to make a normal smart-ass comment. My world had been shattered and I had felt him slipping out of my life just like Tanner had. And I had known our only bond was gone. Forever.

"Bryce?" I asked timidly now, even as I knew the answer.

"Yeah. When did you get back in town?" He asked casually and I could detect boredom in his voice. Just like old times.

"Last weekend. Dad had some work lined up for me. I'm surprised Arick didn't tell you. I thought you were still tight." I was baiting him, I knew he was the beta to Arick's alpha. But I wanted to come across like I hadn't kept up with him or the pack through dad all these years.

"Uh . . ." he started. "I think Arick mentioned it. Just been busy." He sounded embarrassed now but hurried to his next question. "Is your dad there? We need him at the pack house."

My brows knit together now. Fine. No olive branch, I decided. "No, he's on a call. I'll call his cell and let him know. Is it an emergency or can it wait until he's done with his patient?"

I heard Bryce release a breath. "It can wait but I need him to stop by here on his way back. Thanks."

"Sure. See ya around." I said and ended the call. Finally releasing the breath I didn't realize I was holding, I fell on the bed on my back and realized I was clutching the picture in my hand. Frustrated, I glared at it before shoving it into my nightstand and collapsing back on my bed.

Speaking to Bryce took more energy than I cared to admit. Hopefully whatever he needed with my father could be dealt with quickly and we can both go back to pretending neither one exists.

But my gut told me things were different now. I just wasn't sure how.

Chapter Two

Bryce

I looked at my cell as the call flashed a finished time, signaling that Ellie had disconnected. I hadn't been ready to hear from her or talk to her. Shaking my head, I shut off the screen and put the phone down. Her voice had matured but now she still had an "I'm busy" attitude that had replaced the eager tone she'd always had. It had annoyed me then but some small part of me was stung by her not caring I'd called. It irritated me for some reason, even as I tried to shake it off. I could only imagine Arick and I both served as a reminder that Tanner was gone and that was hard enough as his best friend, as his sister it must be even harder.

A soft knock on my office door pulled me from my thoughts as Arick leaned in the office, not entering. "Did you get a hold of Harry?" Arick asked, his brows together in concern. Megan had started her journey into womanhood early and Arick wanted to consult Harry. As two males with no females in the immediate family it seemed the wise thing to do. I shook my head. "No, he was out with a patient. Ellie is going to call his cell."

Arick nodded and started to leave but stopped. "Ellie is back already?"

I leaned forward in my desk chair and ran a hand through my hair. "I guess so. She seemed busy."

Arick walked in now, sitting across from me in a brown leather chair that was soundless as he sunk into it, eyeing me carefully as if considering something. "I think we should invite her to the party in two weeks."

I looked down at my shoes and rubbed the back of my neck. "Do you think that's a good idea?" I wasn't sure why, but the idea put me on edge. Why was this so complicated?

Arick leaned forward and rested his elbows on his knees and steepled his fingers in front of himself. "Why wouldn't it be? We all grew up together."

I was sure smoke was going to come out of my ears while I frantically searched my brain for a good reason why. "I just can't think that wanting to be around her brother's best friends would be pleasant for her." Was the only lame excuse I could find. The truth was while her attitude annoyed me, her lack of doe-eyed stares wasn't something I was ready to deal with. I had resigned myself to single life for all my days as a beta since we seldom married or reproduced and her cold shoulder wasn't something I wanted to deal with all evening. And what if her mate was with her? Or kids? These last thoughts had my chest tightening. Maybe I wasn't ready for Ellie to be an adult. That had to be it, I wanted her to stay the way I remembered her. A friend too young for me and someone to be protected. But my knuckles were clenching on the desk where they rested.

"Like it or not, we were there when her brother died. She's as good as our sister now. And that's family. I'll invite her if you don't want to." Arick's voice told me this wasn't up for discussion, his full alpha voice.

"Okay, fine." I relaxed into my chair, resigning myself to the fact there was no getting around this.

"Good. I'll leave the details to you; I'd like you to be her escort so Megan doesn't get the wrong idea." He stood to leave.

"Wait, what?" I couldn't keep my tone less than confused. So I had to invite her, face shit I didn't want to and babysit? My jaw clenched with frustration. Nope, not on my list of things to do.

"Megan doesn't know who she is and I don't want her to get ideas about Ellie being her new mom like she did the last time I brought a female around." I could see his point but didn't like that this was being put on me.

"Fine, I'll call her later." Maybe I could put it off until Arick forgot about it.

"No, go see her and convince her to come to the party. She's going to resist." Arick ordered in his alpha voice and I took a breath. I couldn't ignore it. Great.

"You're a charmer when you want to be, you can handle it." He said now. As he turned to leave, he stopped and turned back. "Anymore about our mystery biker?"

I shook my head, now really getting angry. How could someone just disappear into thin air? "No, two days and no one has seen anything. Maybe they went to one of the neighboring packs without patrols seeing them. It would be rare, but can happen."

"Just make sure the patrol is taking it seriously, we can't risk a breach with Megan so close to her first shift. They could be trying to get to her to get to us." The worry in his voice had me sitting forward now.

"I agree. I'm going out nightly to make sure they're not missing anything. If that bitch is still around, we'll find her." I assured him.

He nodded slowly and left the office, the door clicking shut behind him.

It was only then I reached into my desk drawer and pulled the flask out. I had been mulling over mentioning it could be someone trying to get the pack leader's daughter, but had wanted to keep it to myself to prevent him from worrying. There had been peace in our sector for several generations, but with the Alpha widowed, it was a show of weakness he hadn't re-mated in 12 years. Only 1 heir, a female who could also be used against him. Too many other Alphas already have tried to form alliances with marriage to Megan, even though she was too young and hadn't even shifted yet.

As I took my first swig from the flask, I welcomed the heat moving up from my belly after the sting on my tongue had eased, and my thoughts began to wander. Megan was like a daughter to me, too. I had been there for her first steps, first words. I was very protective of her and wouldn't let anything happen to her. Not only was it my job as beta to protect her, she was family so it was on me to do it. But now I was stuck babysitting and being a one-man welcoming committee to Ellie.

I went to put the flask back, but as I glanced at the drawer, I saw the picture laying in the bottom. It was of Ellie, Tanner and Harry the day Tanner got his first bike. Arick and I had already gotten our own bikes several months before. Tanner had refused to let us help him save for his. He said he would pay his own money and it would be his baby. I felt a smile tug at my mouth remembering how happy he'd been on that bike, talking for hours about the things he was going to upgrade on it, change on it. I had thought of doing the upgrades myself after Tanner's death but hadn't followed up on it's location since the accident. It could be anywhere now.

Returning the flask and picture to the drawer, I slammed it shut and reached for my jacket. I was in motion and on my bike before the thoughts formed in my head just where I was going.

Time to be the fucking welcoming committee.

Ellie

All burners on the stove were going as I prepared dinner. It was taco Tuesday, so rice, beans and several kinds of meats were all cooking and would be ready about the time Dad got back from the pack house. He said he hadn't eaten a good home cooked meal since I left, so I was going to cook tonight to surprise him. I inhaled the smell over the beef and my mouth started watering. Cooking in this kitchen was muscle memory, I was relieved to find. Dad hadn't changed anything in ten years, so some things had to be replaced or refilled when I got here, but it was easy enough to get the groceries and plan a meal.

A knock at the door drew my attention to the front of the house. I hit the button on the monitor on the counter and the camera was staring at a black leather jacket. I sighed and felt perturbed. I just talked to him on the phone, how could he not take "he's not here" as an answer?

I checked my hair and clothes in the mirror in the hallway on the way down and mentally kicked myself. Bryce had never noticed me, no sense caring now. I opened the door and lost my breath. Bryce had been broad ten years ago, now he was muscular. And bronzed and holy moly those black jeans fit him well. The white cotton shirt under his leather jacket was stretched across his wide chest, his leather jacket was snug on his shoulders and I had a nearly uncontrollable urge to hang off his shoulders by my hands and just feel his strength. His dark hair was still neat and short, because he was as straight laced as he could be. His dark, almost black gaze swung to me and pierced me.

I took two steps back and tried to catch my breath. "Oh, hey Bryce. Dad still isn't here." I said, doing my best to keep my breath steady.

"Uh . . ." he started and then gave a slight shake of his head. "No, that's not why I'm here."

"Oh." Was all I said. Great job, Ellie. You're a real artist of conversation here.

"Arick wanted me to stop by and welcome you back." He said, rubbing the back of his neck like he'd rather be anywhere else and then clasped his hands in front of him.

"That's nice of him. I'll have to call him later. I'm sorry it was pushed off on you." I offered, since he seemed agitated to be standing in my doorway.

"Sorry, that's not what I meant. Just a lot on my mind." He took a deep breath and turned away from me for a minute before facing me again. "Can we talk for a minute? I'd like to catch up."

I opened my mouth to respond but the phone trilled on the table behind me. "That'd be . . . nice. I have to grab that, do you want to come in?" I half hoped he would say no and scurry off. What the other half of me was hoping, I wasn't sure. But either way, I was going to be disappointed.

"How about tomorrow? Coffee at the old diner on route 41?" He asked, his tone almost hopeful. That had been our old hang out since it was right between the high school and the elementary school in town. I did a once over him again before answering. Despite the warning bells sounding off in my head, I forced a weak smile. "I'd like that. Meet you there?"

"Actually, how about if I pick you up here at 1? We can take the bike." He motioned to the black Yamaha down the front steps behind him.

I nodded. "I'll be ready. Thanks for stopping by." I closed the door quickly to reach for the phone, but even as Mrs. Evans prattled on in my ear, I saw his dark shadow hesitate on the other side of the frosted glass before I heard his footsteps go down the steps. After what seemed like a long time and I had gotten Mrs. Evans to agree to a call back from dad, I finally heard the bike start and roll away quickly. Sneaking a peak out the front window, I saw his massive form on the back of the bike. Dressed in all black, he looked powerful as he rode down our gravel driveway to the road before shooting off into the distance. Taking a deep breath and sinking onto the stairs for a minute, I realized my heart had been racing.

I chewed my lip as I replayed the last 20 minutes. That entire encounter had me weirded out and now I was nervous for tomorrow. I don't know why, it was Bryce. My crush was from a lifetime ago and I had been a stupid young girl then. And he clearly didn't seem like he wanted to be here today. So had he only come because of Arick making him drop in? Had Arick even made him?

I was pulled from my thoughts by my cell phone's alert tone chiming. I went to the kitchen and picked it up, shutting off a few of the pots before reading the text.

Dad: I'll be in late. Don't wait up, sweetie.

I typed a quick reply and hit send and sighed. I had made enough food for an army because dad always had a big appetite. I began the arduous task of cleaning up and putting leftovers away, fixing myself a small taco to eat in my room while I watched TV until I fell asleep.

Chapter Three

Ellie

*Moonlight spilled over the field where he stood on the hill. I
saw him. The light danced on his dark fur as his yellow eyes almost
glowed in the night. A chill moved over my skin, waiting to see if he
would come closer. Needing him to come closer.*

*"Ellie," I felt my name move through my mind in his voice.
Was this real? Or was I imagining it?*

*I felt a hunger coming from the wolf on the hill and I knew it
was him. It was Bryce and my body responded, yearning for him to be
near. To change into my own wolf and let her run free by his side . . .*

I sat straight up in bed, sweat breaking across my skin
everywhere. The TV glowed in the corner and the time shone against
the white background. It was after 1 in the morning. I took a
moment to gather my thoughts and take a few deep breaths. Was it
only a dream? I looked at my arms, I still had my clothes on, which
meant I hadn't shifted. It had to be a dream, I decided. I had dreamed
of Bryce as a kid, but nothing this vivid with emotion. I ran a hand
down my hair and reached for the remote near my feet. After clicking
the power off, I went to the window in the darkness to open it and
let the cool air move through the room. But as I looked out over the

field behind my family home, the black wolf stood on the hill just out of the woods that had been there at least all my life. Even at this distance, I saw his yellow eyes glowing. I had seen most of my pack in wolf form, but there was no mistaking Bryce as a wolf. He was the only all-black wolf I had ever seen. His hair as dark as the night around him, given away only by the light of the half-moon that shone off his coat. My hands itched to feel it myself. I yearned to change and go run with him, like we had done many times since my first change. Just like in the dream.

But I stayed rooted to where I was. The dream had gotten into my head and until I calmed my racing heart down, I wasn't going to risk being in a situation where I reacted and made the wrong choice. At that moment, the black wolf put his head down and turned away, disappearing into the trees. As I went back to the bed and laid down on top of the covers, I told myself it was for the best.

The next thing I knew, the morning sun was shining across my floor and up into my face. I blinked at the clock. It was after 9, according to the clock by my bed. I groaned and flopped back on my pillow for just a bit more sleep, but then memories of last night invaded my mind and with the light of day came a new set of questions. Why was Bryce stalking around those woods? And why was he stalking my house? With a surge of conviction for something, not sure what, I got out of bed and headed to shower. As the warm water washed away my night sweat, I kept replaying the dream over and over again in my mind. Had he somehow connected with me while I was sleeping? Normally that only happened between mates after they had mated. The connection in wolf form was only there while both parties were awake, otherwise. And only wolf to wolf. Never wolf to human. As I dried off and put my lotion on, I realized I hadn't heard dad come in, either. That made me frown and make a note to check in his room for him.

I dressed in a simple T-shirt and jeans and pulled my boots on since Bryce said we would take his bike. I'm not sure why he had offered that and why I said it was okay. The thought of being pressed against Bryce for the drive to the diner we used to hang out at really had me on edge. But I had to agree so that he wouldn't know anything was up, like I hadn't had a weird crush on him as a girl, I felt no attraction to him now.

Yeah, right.

I pushed that thought down and went down the hallway to my dad's room. I knocked lightly. "Dad?" I expected to hear some stirring on the other side. But due to the time, he might have already come in and left for the day. It's normal for new pups to be on the way after the harvest moon, which would take a lot of his time. I went downstairs to make coffee because I can't function without caffeine and stood at the kitchen sink staring across the field in the backyard, picturing Bryce there like he was last night. Only this time he was in human form, looking at me with a hunger in his eyes there was no denying.

Okay, where the fuck did that come from? I thought about going upstairs and taking another shower, but very, very cold. It had to be the incoming full moon that had my hormones all messed up. I'll get through this full moon like I always do.

Alone.

With my cup of coffee now in hand, I made my way downstairs to the garage under the house with the large doors that opened to our driveway. I hit the button on my way in and the doors began to roll up and sunlight shone in. Boxes all lined the far wall. It was all my stuff from the city. Tools, belongings I hadn't unpacked yet. I knew behind my boxes were Tanner's belongings that dad had packed up. I wasn't in a rush to face those boxes, even though I had no plans to open them. From where I stood now I could see a T scrawled in Dad's handwriting on one side. Those would likely be moved upstairs into Tanner's old room now that I was turning this into an official garage. I sipped my coffee a few minutes before digging into the first box and unpacking my tools and finding a space for everything. It was soothing, settling into my childhood home. Box by box, I unpacked and decided where things would go; Dad had said this was my space to do with as I pleased. I hadn't missed the hint of pride in his eyes as he showed me the garage he'd had modified with lifts and an engine dolly so I could do real work. And part of me was excited to have a place to call my own instead of going where the latest goon paid me to be to do mods or repairs to their rides. It was good to leave that life behind me.

After some time, I picked my now cold coffee up and drank it while I stared at my brother's bike under the tarp in the corner opposite his boxes. Part of me wanted to see it, another part of me wasn't ready yet. Having to imagine the fear he must have felt staring down those headlights as they approached faster than he could maneuver out of the way. I shuddered and clutched my cup closer with both hands, as if trying to get comfort from it. But I was pulled from my thoughts at the sound of an approaching Yamaha. My heart leapt in my throat as I looked at the analog clock on the far wall behind my brother's bike. It was almost 1. Feeling vulnerable wasn't how I wanted to see Bryce so I cleared my throat and sat my coffee cup aside and grabbed a helmet from the wall as I walked out, pressing the button on the wall to close the doors on my way out.

I used the shield of my helmet to take him in as I buckled it under my chin. He had an all black bike, black boots, black jeans and a black T-shirt. He was wearing his vest instead of his jacket due to the balmy day. He looked ripped and really incredible, I had to admit to myself. But I didn't know if he was seeing someone or had married. I was careful not to mention Bryce or Arick when I talked to my dad on the phone over the last ten years. The jerk of Bryce's chin in my direction as a way of greeting pulled me back to the present. "Ready?" He asked through his helmet.

I nodded and climbed behind him and grasped the tank instead of his hard as-a-rock abs, like Arick had taught me to do. When Bryce noticed my hands on the tank and not him, he looked at me over his shoulder. "Remember how to ride?" He asked and I could hear his smirk in his voice.

I gave a single nod and then we were off. I suspect he rode faster than he needed to on purpose. But if it was just to put distance between us or to try to scare me, I wasn't sure. I do know I was grateful for the distance we were able to put between us as we walked into the diner.

The owner's wife, Janine, came around the counter to greet us. She had aged over the years and wore her silver curls short and tight to her head. Her bright red lipstick curved into a smile as she saw Bryce and I walk in. "Ellie!" She said, throwing her arms around me. "Your dad said you were coming back, but we didn't expect you until next week." I smiled at her warm, cigarette marred voice. "Yeah, I showed up early. Needed to get out of the city." I offered as an explanation.

"I don't blame you. My son hates it. If it weren't for the college, he'd still be here, too. Grab a seat, I'll bring out some coffee. Same as always, Bryce?" She asked, turning her blue gaze to him now. He smiled and nodded. "Please."

She winked at us both. "You got it." And with that, her white orthotics carried her off to the back of the diner. Bryce led us to a booth in the far corner and we sat down. I noticed he positioned himself with his back to the wall and he could see the entire diner behind me and was already surveying.

"Trouble in the pack?" I asked, sliding back in the booth until my back was to the window so I could keep an eye out, too.

He looked at me then, pinning me down with that chocolate gaze. "Just a habit now. I've got to look out for the Alpha."

I nodded and we fell into a silence while Janine delivered our coffee and a slice of apple pie for Bryce. "You want anything to eat, Ellie? Jim's got burgers on now I can have him throw another one on for you."

My stomach growled and I nodded. "That'd be great, thanks. Extra ketchup, please"

She winked at us again and hustled off to another customer on the far side. I shook my head as she walked off. "It's like not much has changed in ten years." I laughed slightly as I added creamer and sugar to my coffee. Bryce watched me before reaching for his pie.

"Yeah, still good old Maple Point. What brought you back?" He asked and then stopped at my sharp glance as I stirred my coffee. Was he on a fact finding mission? My expression made him look away, then clear his throat and start again. "Sorry, that came out wrong. Everyone is excited you're here. It just felt random you decided to come back after all this time. I thought you were pretty settled in the city with your aunt, is all."

I took a deep breath and considered my words before answering. I didn't think the whole town needed to know I was a mechanic for people not on the right side of the law in the city. That I was tired of sleeping with one eye open. And that something was calling me back to here. To home. "College didn't work out like I had hoped and I wasn't sure what I wanted to do. So I figured this was a good place to start. Kind of retrace my steps to see if my plan made sense at all." I took a sip of my steaming coffee.

"What was the plan?" He asked as he ate another bite of pie. I couldn't help but notice the whipped cream at the corner of his mouth, or how he swiped it with his thumb and licked the cream off and then reached for a napkin as he waited for my answer.

I glanced away quickly. *This is not the time, Ellie! You're an adult, not a love-sick teenager!* "Something that wasn't medicine or pack related. I thought I'd go into interior design, but after 2 years of school I got bored and dropped out to save my time and dad's money. Then I met my ex-boyfriend and he taught me some stuff and I freelanced for a bit." I stole a glance at him over my coffee cup at the mention of Matt. Bryce hadn't liked the idea of me dating when we were younger and some part of me was desperate to know if he was still overprotective. But judging by the far off look on his face while he was wiping his fingers on a napkin and looking across the diner at an older couple in the corner told me that was long ago and dead.

He nodded then and was silent for a minute. I realized then he might know his silence put me on edge and was using it to make me anxious and volunteer information. That's what Arick had sent him for. Fact finding. I felt anger rise up on my neck as that realization set in. This wasn't about old friendships. This was about assessing me as a threat. I drank from my coffee for a minute. Damn them both.

Janine dropped off my burger and a mountain of fries and I momentarily forgot my anger as I attacked the fries first. I heard a rumbling across the table and realized Bryce was laughing at me. "What's funny?"

Now he was almost holding his sides as he laughed. I chewed another fry and looked around to see how many people were staring at him losing his mind. After a moment, he wiped a tear from his eye. "You still eat fries like you did when we were kids. It's kind of cute."

I frowned and felt a blush burn my cheeks, not sure if I was offended or not. "Why is that funny?" I demanded, still shoving a fry in my face.

"Come on, Ellie. You grew up and don't look anything like the teenager I remember. Hell, I even took out a picture of you before I saw you yesterday and didn't expect what I saw when you opened the door."

At the thought of him looking at an old photo of me, my eyebrows shot skyward. "That better be a compliment, Bryce." I narrowed my eyes on him.

He leaned back easily and looked me up and down very slowly, and it felt as if he was undressing me in his mind. At least, I felt nude under his gaze. "It was meant as one, I promise." There was a hunger in his eyes that didn't get lost on me, but it was a man looking at a woman and not a boy looking at his friend's sister. I felt heat rise from my chest to my face and I sipped at my coffee to try to hide it.

"So," Bryce said, leaning forward. "In town for good? Or just until you figure things out?"

I felt my eyes narrow. "Does it matter either way?" I asked now.

"Yeah, as Beta I look out for the pack, too. We usually keep tabs on who's in the territory." He said calmly, also sipping at his coffee.

"Don't worry," I said, picking up my burger. "I won't get in the way of pack business."

"That's not-" His sentence stopped as his cell began ringing in his pocket. "I've got to take this, just a sec." He stepped away from the table and I ate in silence as he took the call. I felt so angry with myself for thinking this was a social call. It was just fact-finding. Pack business. Iciness moved through me. I was no longer a friend's sister. I was pack business. I finished my burger while he was on the phone and sat back, full but still in a shitty mood.

Bryce came back to the table still on his phone, but the expression on his face made me concerned. It was worry, it was fear, it was . . . not good.

"Okay, I'll be right there." He ended the call and put the phone back in his pocket. "We've got to go. I think you should go with me." He dropped cash on the table before I could protest and grabbed my hand to help me out of the booth. Janine called out as we left, but he was pulling me behind him. "What is it?" I ask. "I'll explain when we get there." The placation in his tone angered me. That line had been used on me a lot as a teenager. I yanked my arm from his hand and crossed my arms. "No, I'm not a child. What is going on?" I demanded. Squinting against the bright sunlight now.

He sighed after swinging astride his bike. "Did your dad get home yesterday?" He was pulling his gloves on. As his words registered with me, my arms fell at my side. "I don't know. He texted me right after you left yesterday afternoon and said to not wait up. It's normal this time of year for him to be out at all hours with new pups on the way. Why do you ask? Did something happen?" My heart was pounding now, dreading what I would hear next.

He looked away for a moment before meeting my gaze. "They just found his truck at the corner of our territory. He wasn't with it."

Bryce

I was trying very hard not to think about the huge breasts mashed against my back or the gorgeous blonde they belonged to sitting behind me. Yesterday had taken me totally by surprise as she opened the door and then stepped back when she realized it was me. Her tits had bounced under her button down shirt and her silver hair tumbled around her shoulders in sexy waves. Her curves had filled out and seeing her dig into those fries and the burger like she had only told me her appetite had finally caught up to her and filled her out.

Too many times while we sat at the diner today, I had to shift and adjust my zipper thinking about how she would fill my hands as I pulled her to my face. All of her to my face.

I tried to think of ice and cold showers as my dick started to come to life thinking about how all of her would taste. Instead I thought of the fact that she remembered how to ride on the back of a motorcycle and wondered if that's what Arick had taught her the one time he had taken her out on his. Or if someone in the city had. She had mentioned an ex-boyfriend. The thought of anyone touching her or teaching her how to do anything that would put her in direct contact with someone made my wrist twist on the throttle and push the bike faster as we went down the 2-lane county road toward the edge of the Shadow Wolf territory.

I was able to shift my thoughts to where we were going. The doctor just disappearing and near the edge of the territory could mean that a renegade had gotten to him. And that may mean that something bad was about to happen. The pack had to have a doctor to care for them in the event that there was a territory war. A human doctor wouldn't be able to heal a wolf shifter, humans couldn't even know we exist unless they were trusted.

I slowed as we neared the area where our borderlines were guarded. Damon stepped up to the bike and nodded. He was wearing just jeans, which means they likely tracked the smell of the doctor to his truck or beyond. We came to a stop and Ellie hopped off the bike quickly and removed her helmet. Her silver curls fell down around her shoulder and Damon cleared his throat. "Ellie," he said.

She smiled "Hey, Damon. Long time, no see." She looked him over and I felt a fist form and leaned back on the bike and hooked my hands on the neck of my vest to keep from punching something. Or someone.

"What did you find, Damon?" I could hear anger in my voice but didn't try to squelch it or explain. I was angry, but fuck if I knew why.

He turned and pointed over the hill. "The doctor's truck is back there. The keys are in it. The driver's side door was open and there wasn't anyone around. It doesn't look like anything was taken. His bag is still there. So I tracked his scent as far as I could. I lost it in the Diablo territory."

I heard Ellie gasp. "He wouldn't have gone over there. Navarro hates us." She said and her voice broke. I looked at her then as she held her helmet under her arm, holding it so tight her hands were white. "Could I see the truck?" She asked. I nodded and climbed off the bike and removed my helmet and left it with the bike. Damon led us through tall grass and wild flowers and as he went to the top of the hill, I couldn't help but thinking this was my fault for not finding that bitch on the bike sooner. I started to ask if her father had been seeing someone, thinking maybe it was the doctor's girlfriend. But I thought better of it. This wasn't the time. She already seemed angry with all the questions at the diner. I'm not sure why, but I just wanted to know everything, where she had been, who she had seen, what brought her back? All of it. There was a hunger deep in me for reasons I couldn't explain.

As we crested the hill, Ellie cried out and started running to the white pickup truck parked near the edge of the woods. I frowned as I looked around. These are the same woods that back up to Harry's land. I was in these woods last night and hadn't seen this truck or any sign of anyone. That means it had come here this morning. She threw her helmet in the passenger seat and started searching the truck for something. Frowning, I watched her. She grabbed Harry's bag and opened it. "All the pain killers are gone." She handed me the bag to see and then went to the front of the truck. She opened the hood and felt near the engine. "It's still warm, he hasn't been gone long." I saw the worry on her face as she looked around and caught her lip between teeth. "He might come back to it. I don't see his phone anywhere. Maybe he's bringing medicine to the Diablo pack?" She suggested.

I doubted it. Our doctors weren't allowed to cross territory without Alpha or beta approval. I pulled my cell phone out and dialed the pack house. "Mr. Bryce," was the cold greeting I got from the guard at the entrance to the pack house. "Did Doctor Savoy show up for Megan yesterday?" I asked.

"He didn't sign in, no." Was the short answer. I thanked her and ended the call. "He never went to the pack house yesterday. I was on patrol in those woods last night, I didn't see or sense anyone or anything."

My head was racing and my heart was keeping up. This was a bunch of "not good" wrapped up in a neat bow. With Megan's shift coming up soon, the pack would be focused on her and distracted, which primed us to be targets.

Ellie came to stand in front of me. "Why were you in the woods last night?" She asked now, staring me in the eyes. Her blue eyes told me she had seen me last night. In addition to needing to up the patrol until we found that biker, I had wanted to answer a question. I had reached out to her mind. I don't know what prompted me to wonder if she was my mate. Betas seldom mated, but something told me to reach out. The fact that she hadn't responded meant she wasn't my mate. So I would now do my best to keep my distance I had decided, but with her dad taking off for enemy lines that might be harder than I first thought.

"Well?" She prompted, pulling me from my thoughts.

"Patrols are higher than normal. Just doing my pack job." I answered sharply. She narrowed her eyes, but turned away from me and looked over the field. "I suppose going into Diablo territory is out of the question?" She asked.

"Completely. I have to get Arick involved now."

She nodded thoughtfully. "Makes sense. They obviously took him for something."

I didn't want to point out that there was no sign of a struggle and everything was left behind except his cell, which means that he could have made a deal to get out of our territory, which may have something to do with the biker I saw the other day.

"I'll take you home and get back to the pack house." I barked out the order and grabbed her elbow to get her out of here. "Damon, alert the others. We're upping our patrols along this border. I want more dogs out here within earshot of each other."

Ellie yanked her arm away from me. "Hold on, Mr. Beta, SIR." She sneered. "I'll take Dad's truck home." Without waiting for me to agree or not, she climbed in and slammed the door shut and before I could protest, took off across the field toward the road, churning up grass and flowers in her wake.

"She's not changed a bit." Damon said with a half-laugh, running a hand through his hair and watching the truck disappear into the distance.

I shook my head as I watched her disappear. "No, she hasn't." Was all I could say, feeling somehow hollow without her near. Damon turned to me then and squinted in the sun looking at me. I was taller than he was and it was a sunny, hot day. "Is she seeing anyone?"

I balled my fist up and went back to my bike, swinging stride it before answering. "She's off limits until we figure out what the fuck is going on here, Damon. Stay away." He saluted me and I peeled out, really pissed off now.

Ellie

I threw my phone on the passenger seat beside me as I got Dad's voicemail again. Anxiety clawed at my throat as I sped down the road to our house. This wasn't like him at all to just up and disappear without a word or a call or a note or something.

Pulling up into the driveway, the truck hadn't completely stopped moving when I slammed it into park and jumped out of the cab, running into the house. I punched in the number code on the lock and started down the hallway to my father's office. Inside, my senses were assaulted with smells I hadn't smelled in years. I had been careful not to come in here, remembering the many times Tanner and I had barged in on dad working on paperwork begging him for the latest toy, to go fishing in the creek, to spend time with him, or asking him what's for dinner. He would always smile, a smile that crinkled the corner of his eyes and took a sip from whatever drink he had poured himself as he looked at us over the rim of the glass before teasing us and ultimately giving us what we wanted. I stood in front of his desk and forced my fists to unclench as I took a deep breath and smelled the leather and slight tobacco smell that I wasn't sure where it came from because my father didn't smoke or chew. It may have been one of the liquors in the cabinet. I moved behind the desk and began opening drawers and shifting papers around, looking for something that would tell me where he had been. No patient schedule, no notes taken by the phone on top of his desk, the computer wasn't logged in and I didn't know the password. I sat down and stared at the screen for a minute, wondering if I could figure it out. My hands hovered over the keyboard when I heard something, someone walking down the hall toward me. Searching around for something sharp, I opened the drawer in front of me and found a Taurus in the drawer. I grabbed it, confirmed there was a bullet in the chamber and waited.

I felt my shoulders visibly relax as Bryce filled the doorway to my father's study. "Find anything?" He asked as he leaned against the door frame, folding his arms across his massive chest. I guessed he had left his vest on his bike because he only wore his black T-shirt and I couldn't help but notice how that shirt was stretched tight against his muscles. I stiffened my spine and sniffed before putting the gun back, not sure what I would have done if I'd had to use it. I heard his laugh. "Were you going to shoot me?"

Indignant with his stupid question, I clicked the safety back on and deposited the gun in the drawer, slamming it shut. "My father is missing, in case you hadn't gathered that from his truck being left in a field in the middle of nowhere. I have no idea what's going on," I stopped there, sweeping my gaze over him before adding "No idea who to trust."

His arms went to his side as he stalked forward to stand in front of the desk. "What the hell is that supposed to mean?" Now he sounded angry and the nerve at his right temple was ticking.

"It means you showed up at my house last night in the field and now my father is missing after you got me out of the house. How do I know you didn't have your goons come dig around trying to find something?" Now I was out of the chair, leaning on the desk, doing my best to keep my temper in check.

He leaned down on his hands on the desk. "Well, you even admitted you showed up early and now the old man is missing. How do I know you didn't have something to do with it?"

I straightened and threw my head back in a humorless laugh. "Oh, you got me, Sherlock! I took my father's truck to rush back here and toss the place looking for something, but I don't know what. But wait, there's more! I agreed to coffee with you so I had an airtight alibi when your guards found his truck just abandoned in the field!"

He straightened and those damn arms folded across his chest again and I saw the tattoo peeking out from under the sleeve of his shirt. "I don't think you know how plausible that sounds. It's certainly suspicious you showed up early unannounced and now he's missing and his pain pills are gone, too."

I folded my arms over my chest to keep from slapping him. "Get out of my house," I finally say low and slow, determined he wasn't going to get me to fly off the handle like he was trying to.

"It's on pack property, I'll stay if I want to." He sauntered around the desk to stand in front of me. "I'll do anything I damn well please." He says, but I heard his breath catch in his throat as mine stops all together. He was really close and now all I could smell was him. Earthy, like Pine and cedar with exhaust and gasoline. This was too dangerous. I still didn't know what was happening here, my father was missing and every time I turned around, Bryce was there. Seemingly against his will. That didn't change that he was really in my space and I was rattled. But I wasn't sure how to not show that, so without thinking I chewed on my bottom lip.

He grasped my chin and I was forced to meet his dark eyes now. "Don't chew your lip. It's too beautiful to do anything other than be kissed."

Shocked by his words as heat shot through me, I released my lip. "What the he-" I began only for his mouth to crash against mine. His hand moved from my chin to grasp my neck to make sure I didn't move away from him. The other circled my waist until he pulled me close and I felt my breasts mash against his chest, which drew a groan from us both. He kissed my bottom lip first before pushing my jaw open with his thumb to allow his tongue in. With a whimper, I let him in. Tasting him. Coffee, sweat and frustration. But frustration at what? Determined I was going to rattle him as much as he rattled me, I pulled his shirt out of his jeans, seeking skin. He was burning under my touch as my hand moved across an incredible amount of muscle, scars and him. I felt in that moment that stepping into him wouldn't ever get me close enough. I felt his hard-on against my belly and knew I still wanted him. Only now I could name my need as a woman and not question what it was as a young girl. This was primal, it was deep. It was the strongest pull I had ever felt. Even with Matt it hadn't been like this. I felt dizzy with need and all I could do was moan and whimper as his hands moved to my breasts and his thumbs moved across my nipples through my bra and shirt. I flexed my hips against his leg, needing the contact to go on, to get closer. There was a shrill ringing and at first I thought it was in my ears until he broke the contact and I realized his cell phone was going off. Someone was calling him. I jumped away from him like a kid caught necking in the living room and straightened my shirt.

He watched me but didn't bother straightening his shirt as he took the phone from his pocket and answered it while his eyes stayed locked on me. "Yeah?" he said to the phone.

While whomever was on the other end talked, I picked up my father's desk phone and dialed his cell number again. When it went straight to voicemail, I replaced the receiver, my spirits sinking even farther.

"That makes sense," Bryce was saying now. "I'll ask her." I met his gaze at the term "her." Her who? I felt jealousy rearing its ugly head like it had when we were younger. The three amigos had never wanted for female companionship and I was sure that hadn't changed over the years.

He returned the phone to his pocket and then straightened his shirt, finally. "Arick wants to know if you could come help Megan." He explained, leaning against the bookcase to his right. "She's due to shift soon and she's got woman troubles going on. Which is why we asked your dad to stop in yesterday."

I took a deep breath while considering. I remember Megan as a baby, her dark good looks inherited from her mother, Sarah. My heart had broken for the baby, knowing what it's like to grow up without a mom around. Mine hadn't died, just taken off and left my father to raise two children with shifter capabilities. "Is it safe to have me at the pack house after just accusing me of mutiny of some kind?" I said, my tone slightly bitchy. Okay, bitchier than I wanted. But I hadn't forgotten what he had just said before turning my body into a puddle of goo. I half expected an apology but was disappointed. He raked a hand through his hair as a half-smile played with his full lips before returning his gaze to mine. "Yes, security will sign you in and out and we have guards posted throughout the house to protect Megan."

Okay, now I'm pissed. "Are you flipping kidding me right now, Bryce? My brother grew up with you and Arick, we were practically all family and you really think I'd have nefarious intentions toward the pack?" My voice sounded more hurt than angry and that annoyed me. I didn't want this asshole to think he could hurt me.

This time his shoulders relaxed and his hands fell to his side. "I can't take chances, Ellie. I'm the beta and my first priority is this pack's safety. Do you want to ride with me? Or are you coming in your own car?"

My hand itched to slap the shit of him and I made a snap judgement to put distance between us both. "I'll drive myself. I have to pick some things up."

"What things?" He seemed like he was back on his guard.

I rolled my eyes. "For Megan, blockhead. None of your business. The goons can check it when I get to the house." I turned back to the desk, dismissing him with a hand wave.

At my comment, he kind of chuckled and started for the door. "When should I tell Megan to expect you?" He asked over his shoulder, stopping in his tracks but not turning to face me.

I chewed my lip as I considered my answer. "I'll be along in the next few hours."

He nodded then and I was left to my thoughts. Sadly, they were all consumed by what we'd just shared and what he had almost out right accused me of.

How could he think I had anything to do with what happened to my father? Whatever the hell that turned out to be? I sunk into the chair behind his desk again and held my head in my hands, wracking my brain trying to figure out just what the hell was happening here. I came home to root myself and find clarity. Not to have my father turn up missing and being kissed by a childhood crush in my father's study. This was not the plan, I told myself again. I was so disgusted with how things were slipping out of my control, I stood quickly and moved to my father's liquor cabinet in the corner. I poured myself a shot of scotch and downed it quickly and made a note to buy a few bottles of something other than scotch.

Something told me I was going to need it.

Chapter Four

Bryce

The bulge in my jeans hadn't relented the entire way home and I replayed this afternoon in my mind for the hundredth time, trying to forget how Ellie's body felt against mine, how right we felt together. As a beta, we didn't always mate. But then I had to ask why hadn't Ellie found her mate yet? Was it Matt? Is that why she came back to Maple Point?

And then there was the mystery biker, the disappearance of Harry and this crazy attraction I felt to Ellie, even though she wasn't my mate, if I even had one. I shook my head to clear it and moved from the window in my office to sit behind the desk. Harry disappearing had me on edge. The few spies we had in the Navarro pack were digging, but so far nothing had turned up yet. But it had only been a few hours. The pack supplied all of Harry's medicines, so what would he have to gain by selling some to Navarro's group? The rules were that all property changing pack hands had to be cleared by the Alpha. Arick had confirmed not getting any requests from anyone let alone Harry. And why had Harry just left his truck like that?

A knock at the door pulled me from my thoughts. Before I could answer Arick's father, Grayson poked his head around the door. "Oh, sorry to interrupt." He said, though he was clearly not. "Have you seen Arick?"

Blinking a few times to clear my thoughts, I shook my head. "No, he was with Megan the last I saw him. They were out back near the pond."

I looked at Grayson, noticing the age creeping in beside his eyes as silver touched the temples of his short blonde hair. His appearance was more of a military man than an Alpha in my opinion. He wasn't much older than Arick, having become a father when he was just a teenager with his mate, Etta. He had stepped down when Arick turned 21, which was tradition and handed the pack, and all its responsibilities, over to Arick and I. But he still stayed close in case we needed help or guidance. As we navigated the loss of our friend while we were named Alpha and Beta, he had been invaluable and supportive.

He nodded now and left without another word. I frowned at that. Normally he asked me for the latest goings-ons around the pack but he didn't this time. It could be he had already heard everything from Arick, hence why he was there asking for him. My thoughts scattered and my heart started racing blood through my body when I heard a car come to a stop in front of the house, sure it was Ellie with the things she had brought Megan. Shaking my head to clear it, I worked my way to the front of the house as the maid opened the door. Ellie stood there and I felt the air whoosh out of my lungs as she stood there in a low-cut shirt under her open leather jacket and her tight blue jeans hugging every inch of her thick curves.

I wanted to feel those curves against me again, I realized. Clearing my throat, she shifted her gaze to mine. "Brought the stuff." She said, lifting the small backpack in her hand with a sardonic smile. "Wanna search it?" And then she smirked "or me?" She challenged me with an arched brow. She needed to stop that, I noted as I frowned. It was too fucking adorable. "Your clothes don't leave anything to the damn imagination, so that won't be necessary." I glanced at the maid, Miranda. Her face was pinched with concern and she was looking at me with her aged brown eyes as she waited for my instruction. Miranda had been around the entire time I had been a child, but she must not remember Ellie. With a curt nod from me, she moved to let Ellie in. "I think Megan is back here." And I turned to walk stiffly toward the back of the house. So Ellie thought she was a smart ass? I cracked my knuckles as I thought about how fun it would be to show her not to mess with the big boys and I felt my wolf growl deep in my soul with a feral frenzy. Yes, we'd both enjoy it.

I opened the patio doors off the kitchen and we stepped out onto the terrace. The red brick led out to a large back yard surrounded by weeping willows that hung low to the ground. The area was lush and green and it wasn't lost on me how nice it looked, I just didn't care today.

I scanned the yard and heard a laugh coming from my right. My gaze swept in that direction and saw Arick and Megan down by the pond as a duck waddled up to them. I looked at Ellie and nodded that way with my chin and let her take the lead. As I followed her, I couldn't keep my eyes from staring at her ass and I realized I had seen that same ass before.

"Do you ride, Ellie?" I asked, putting my hands in my pocket to keep from touching her.

She spoke over her shoulder as we continued to walk. "Yes, I have a black CBR. Why?"

I didn't really know how to respond because I had expected her to lie about it. She stopped then and turned to face me, a look of realization on her face. "You don't remember seeing me a few days ago?" All I could do was blink at her. "Uh . . ." she started laughing. "Oh my God! You didn't realize that was me! Who did you think it was? The boogie man?"

Her laugh was extremely melodic, but I was fighting with several different emotions. Confusion, slight amusement and anger. All at the same time. Thankfully, Arick and Megan walked up then. But as Arick looked at her laughing at me and then my frustrated face, he was apparently as lost as I was.

"Hey, Ellie." He finally spoke. She took a few deep breaths and smiled at him. "Hey, Arick. Long time no see!" She jumped at him and for a moment I was on my guard, wondering her next move. But then she threw her arms around his neck as he swung her around like he had done when she was younger. He was over 6 feet so her feet only came to his shins as she dangled from his neck and the look of pure joy on her face at seeing him had my teeth on edge. "Okay, that's enough," I finally said and Arick set Ellie down on the ground with eyes narrowed at me. Shit, he was going to ask me about that later.

"You really need to calm down, grumpy." Ellie said now, wrinkling her nose at me. I felt myself relax the slightest at the adorable gesture. But then I glanced at Megan and tensed up again. Megan was staring at Ellie from her leather jacket to her silver hair to her jeans and boots and back again. "You must be Ellie," Megan finally spoke. Ellie smiled and nodded. "I am. But I haven't seen you since you were a baby. You're almost as tall as me!" Megan's face split in a large grin, revealing her braces. "I am 12. But taller than most people in my class." Arick spoke up now, his bearded jaw tense. "I'm already having trouble keeping boys at bay. Now that she's growing up it's going to be even more difficult." I stood watching the exchange, feeling a sense of familiarity that I didn't want to. I still didn't know what Ellie's motivations were for being back in town. But Arick seemed to trust her so there was no arguing with him at this point. I just had to make sure my guard stayed up. But the unadulterated hero worship in Megan's eyes as she looked at Ellie told me I was in a world of trouble.

Ellie

Arick had led us up to Megan's room for me to help answer her questions about her time and how to prepare for the next one in a month's time. I was painfully aware that Bryce was on the other side of the door, waiting for me to make a bad move toward Megan. The knowledge made me feel pissy and hurt at the same time. But as I looked at her now, her dark tan skin and black hair falling around her shoulders in tight messy curls, I felt an odd protective sense come over me. This poor girl had grown up without a mother and had gotten herself to adolescence with just two overbearing males in her life. She had grit to her, I had to admit it as I looked around us. Her room was decorated a soft powder pink with orange accents and twinkle lights. Photos were scattered around the wall, haphazardly taped to the wall wherever the mood had struck her. She had a fluffy canopy bed complete with pink, frilly curtains where we sat side by side on the edge now.

"Thank you for helping me today, Ellie. I know your dad is the doctor but it felt so much better having a girl to talk to." She fell quiet for a moment, staring at her hands. When she finally spoke, she was extremely quiet "I heard Dad say your dad is missing." She began.

I nodded hesitantly, not sure where this was going. "That's right. I'm really worried about him."

Megan nodded and then looked at me, her eyes shimmering with tears. "I don't know what I'd do if it was my dad. I'd be so lost without him." I put my arm around her shoulders, knowing what it's like when you realize that the people you count on to be in your life aren't necessarily going to be around forever. "I know what you mean. But you have your Uncle Bryce to protect you, too."

Megan rolled her eyes and laughed. "Puh-lease! He's so ridiculous! He won't let any of my friends come over unless they're girls. Dad said it was fine, but Uncle Bryce is so unfair!" She huffed.

There was a knock at the door and Bryce called out "I can still hear you."

Megan and I shared a knowing look and began giggling. We fell back on the bed then, staring up at the lights and curtains around the bed. "This is a pretty bed," I said, feeling the soft duvet under my hand. "Yeah," Megan said. "But I think I want to change it. I don't think dad will let me, though."

I frowned, but didn't look at her. "Why not?"

Megan propped herself up on her elbow and looked down at me. "I don't think he's ready for me to grow up. All anyone can talk

~ 51 ~

about is my birthday party and my first shift." She chewed on her lips for a minute and I waited for her to continue. "What if I don't shift? What if the party is for nothing?"

I rolled and faced her, propping myself up on my side and placing my head on my hand. "Well," I said. "It's okay if you don't shift. The party is to celebrate you turning 12. It just happens to line up with your *expected* first shift. Your dad is still going to be crazy about you whether you shift or not." I tucked a small chunk of hair behind her ear.

Megan laughed then. "Dad is just crazy."

We both giggled. "Still, though. I've known your dad since I was a baby. He'll still love you."

Megan turned those sharp eyes at me again. "Have you known Uncle Bryce that long, too?"

I lowered my eyes, really hoping she wouldn't ask about my relationship with Bryce. "Yes. He and your dad were best friends with my brother."

"What happened?" Megan asked, drilling into me with her gaze. This kid was relentless.

"My brother passed away and I went to live with my aunt." I answered, lowering my eyes.

"Why?" Again, more questions.

I took a slow, deep breath. "It was really hard being in the house where my brother had lived and knowing he wasn't coming home anymore." My vision blurred with tears at the pain piercing my heart. It hadn't gotten better over the years, just easier to push aside.

Megan flopped over and wrapped her arms around me. "I'm sorry. I'll ask dad if I can be your family now."

I laughed and she smiled up at me. "It's okay, I've been like a little sister to them for a really long time. I used to annoy them so much when we were younger."

"Like how?"

I hadn't thought of Megan being an only child and not understanding having a younger sibling trying to tag along all the time. "Well," I hesitated. "Like when my brother got his first motorcycle. Your dad took me for a ride to try to get me to feel included. Bryce and my brother were so mad. They thought it wasn't safe for me to ride, even with someone as accomplished and safe as your dad. And then as they got older, they wanted to talk to girls, and I was just always there. My dad counted on my brother to help me get to and from school safely, so I was always at places I wasn't necessarily welcome." I winked at her then.

"I do that to Daddy now. He catches me trying to learn pack business outside his office and tells me that it's not something I need to worry about." As a female, Megan's husband should inherit the pack, according to the order of things.

Megan sat up, a realization coming across her face. "That means you knew my mom, too. What was she like?"

I was silent for a moment as I brought all the memories of Sarah I had to mind. "She was kind and handled your dad's outrageous ideas really well. Almost like a queen. She would have been good to help lead the pack. Your mom and dad were older than I was and I was around because of my brother. So I didn't see your dad and your mom interact a lot, but they loved each other. And they both loved you more than anything in the world."

Megan's eyes dropped from my face. "I wish I could remember her."

I put a hand on Megan's shoulder. "You were just a baby. But I know she'd be really proud of you and adore you and she'd be proud of how your dad has raised you." I offered a reassuring smile.

Just then there was a quick knock at the door and it opened. I recognized Arick's father from when we were younger. He had aged extremely well, still tan and blonde. His hair had started to go white at his temples. His green eyes rested on me as he walked into the room. "Oh, my apologies, Megan. I didn't know you had company."

"That's okay, grandpa. This is Ellie, a friend of my dad's."

"Mr. Vargulf," I greeted as we both sat up in the bed and I scooted to the edge, completely uncomfortable as his eyes raked over me from head to toe and back again. He looked like he was about to begin rubbing his hands together.

"Hello, Ellie. It's been a long time," he said quietly. "Arick was just filling me in about your father. I'm really sorry."

My chin came up. "Thank you. We don't know what's happened, but I'm sure I'll figure it all out and everything will be fine." I offered a weak smile, to which he nodded.

"I see. Uh, Megan? I'm getting ready to leave and just wanted to say goodbye. Give grandpa a kiss."

Megan scooted off the bed and did as she was told, but Grayson embraced her, he held my eyes the entire time and I felt naked under his gaze. It was unnerving.

After Megan backed away from him, he nodded in my direction. "Good seeing you again, Ellie." And he left, brushing past Bryce who had an unreadable expression on his face as he came to lean on the door frame, like he had done at my house.

"All set?" Bryce asked Megan. She nodded at him. "Yes, I think I'm okay." Megan said before turning to me. "Are you joining us for the evening meal, Ellie?" I looked back to Bryce and his eyes were intently on me. "I'd love that. It'll give me a chance to catch up with your dad." Bryce sucked in a breath and stiffened, but I didn't care. The jerk kissed me until I was senseless and then wanted me gone? He could get over himself.

We walked down the stairs in silence, but I was painfully aware of Bryce's gaze on me the entire time. He seemed really upset that he didn't recognize me the other day on the bike, but I had changed a lot in ten years. Maybe if he hadn't had his head up his ass, he would have been given a chance to realize it sooner. But no, he had to be big-bad-beta. Dick.

The dining hall was already set and food was coming out of the kitchen. We stood until Arick came in and sat down. He hadn't changed much in ten years, I noticed. His sandy blond hair was still long, pulled back in a ponytail today instead of his usual bun. His beard was almost rust colored and trimmed close to his face. He did have more tattoos than I remembered, though. Now they were all the way down his arm to his fingers. Rings decorated several fingers and his watch was large and twinkled in the light of the dining hall.

He sat down and then we all sat. In addition to the four of us was Arick's head of security Jason and Damon. We all sat quietly while food was served and then Jason cleared his throat. Jason was older than Arick by almost a decade. His white hair was cropped close to his head and his crystal blue eyes missed nothing. He was bigger than I remembered, his tank stretched tight across pecs that were also heavily tattooed. "So, Ellie. I heard you were back in town. Settling in all right?"

I nodded. "Yes, Arick sent the welcoming committee to greet me." I smirked at Bryce. "But I'm just about settled. Once dad is found things can get back to normal quickly."

Jason nodded. "We've increased patrols on both sides in case someone knows something. The town has been combed. We'll find him and bring him home safely." I sighed with relief inwardly. I knew my father had a lot of loyal patients but his sudden disappearance did seem extremely suspicious so I appreciated the continued loyalty.

Damon chimed in now. "It was odd how his truck was just left there in the clearing with the driver's door opened. Alpha, have you talked to the Navarro pack?"

Arick shook his head. "Father is handling it since he and Sal go way back. He'll handle it tomorrow, he said. We should know something by the evening." That brought me little comfort. For some reason, I didn't trust Grayson. He had always set me on edge but now it was even worse and I could hear my wolf growl in my head at the mention of the previous Alpha.

"Interestingly enough," Bryce said now. "The rider I was looking for was Ellie."

I looked at him now, daring him to explain further. He sounded so angry, and I would be angry too if I was an obnoxious asshat. Jason laughed at this and Damon smiled.

"So," Jason said. "The rider you had us searching the territory for was here all along?"

Bryce cleared his throat. "In my defense, I hadn't seen her in ten years and didn't know she was still into motorcycles."

I waved him off. "Not much has changed about me in the last decade. Still little old me." I said sweetly, a coy smile playing with the corners of my mouth. From the white knuckled grip he had on his glass, I could tell he was on edge and all the warning signs were there. But I was having fun poking the bear. "But it's incredibly sweet of you to be sweeping the entire territory for me. I'll need to add that to my resume as a highly sought-after rider."

Arick laughed at this and we settled into the meal making small talk and catching up. Bryce didn't really seem to eat, instead choosing to keep me pinned where I was with his gaze. I ignored him, deliberately trying to provoke him by laughing too much at Damon's terrible jokes. The reaction I wanted was there, the white knuckles and grunts were proof enough. After the meal, Arick looked outside. "It would be a nice night for a fire, Damon. Get one started for us."

Damon nodded and left the table. Arick turned to me then. "Join us?"

I nodded as I stood. "Sure."

"What about me, Daddy?" Megan asked, already at my side.

"You need to sleep. Especially with everything going on. Go ahead upstairs and I'll be there to tuck you in shortly."

Megan's head dropped and her face flamed. She was embarrassed, but knew better than to argue with her father. But she perked back up. "Can we invite Ellie to my party in two weeks?" Megan asked, steepling her fingers under her chin hopefully.

I opened my mouth to protest "Oh, I don't-"

"Arick actually wanted me to ask," Bryce interrupted, looking at me. "It just didn't come up while we were at coffee earlier."

Megan turned to me. "Please come, Ellie? It'll be so fun! I have all of the decorating to do the day before and if you want to help, you can come help or just show up and have fun and eat lots of food." She paused to giggle. "I have so much food planned for the party. Uncle Bryce can really put away some finger foods." She was smiling at me now and I was really helpless to resist her chocolate eyes. I smiled at her. "I'd love to. And I'll help with the decorations, too." She threw her arms around me and I smiled wider. "It's going to be great!"

"I'm sure it'll be fun. You have my number if you need anything. Feel free to call day or night." I said to her as she left the dining room. Glancing at Arick, I smiled a sad smile. "She's a lot like her mother." I remembered Sarah as incredibly willful and strong. She had given Arick a lot of headaches but they had loved each other dearly. Arick returned my sad smile as he looked away. "She reminds me of her mother every day. I wish she could have seen how she's turning out."

I offered a friendly hand on his shoulder as he stood to leave the dining room. "You're doing a great job. She would be really proud of you."

I heard a low growl behind me and my head whipped around to see Bryce's face looking evil and ready to snap. I swallowed and slowly removed my hand from Arick's shoulder and his face eased but he still looked mad. Arick looked between us and cleared his throat. "Thank you. We're both nervous for her first shift. Sarah's was difficult."

From the table we went out to the back of the house and off the patio Damon had a large bonfire burning down by the pond where Arick and Megan had been feeding ducks earlier. The flames were bright and licked the night sky, dancing for the half moon high in the sky.

Chairs were scattered about around the fire and I took one, enjoying the warmth of the fire against the nip of the air. I didn't sit long before I was transfixed by the flames. Arick sat at my side, also just silent for some time. This felt comfortable, like it had when we were kids. As if no time had passed and I just let the nostalgia wash over me for a few moments. But something made my eyes begin wondering and drew my attention on the other side of the fire. My gaze clashed with Bryce's as he stared me down. I couldn't pinpoint his expression, but it made me uneasy. I blinked a few times to break the contact and took a breath before looking at Arick. "Do you enjoy being Alpha? The pack seems to be doing well."

Arick chuckled, not looking away from the fire. "I feel like I'm good at it. But it's a large responsibility. Now with that construction project at the corner of town getting underway soon I'll be even busier. We have to figure out security for the pack while it's being constructed and what we'll do if humans move in and they don't know about us."

I nodded. We had some allies in the human world, but not everyone knew what we were. The best-case scenario they dismissed us as wild wolves they spotted at night. But that didn't stop some of them from hunting us, either. So I could imagine how that would impact the security of the pack. "When is it supposed to be done?" I asked, just to keep the conversation going.

"Father is handling it. Probably in the next few years. They haven't even broken ground. Some kind of red tape. I'm not as close to it as I should be as alpha. But if father said he's handling it, I'm glad it's out of my hands for a while." I remembered it being a topic of debate a long time before I left. I couldn't believe after a decade nothing had moved forward.

We talked some more about things that had been happening around the pack, who had moved on and who was still in Maple Springs. It should have helped ease my tension, but as the night ticked on, I only felt more on edge and I knew I had to get out of there soon. I couldn't get my father off my mind and Bryce was staring holes into me that made me feel like swiss cheese.

"I should be going," I said finally once the conversation lulled and stood.

Bryce was next to me in an instant. "I'll see you out." Arick and I said good night and I started back up the patio to the house. I tried not to give in to the urge to goad him any further but I was painfully aware of him not far behind me. I opened the front door before Bryce or the maid had a chance to. Bryce looked outside and let out a low whistle. "That's your car?" He asked and I smiled at the tone of his voice. He was impressed.

It was a white GTR, with aftermarket mods, special black wheels and a spoiler. I had swapped a tighter fly wheel on it to make it more sensitive to shifting and replaced the intake system. It had been my first car in the city and I had just kept it up, changing things as they needed and maintained it. "Yeah," I said lamely. "That's my baby."

We walked down the steps and when I would have reached for the door of my car, he put a hand on my wrist. "I still have questions for you."

I looked him up and down without moving my chin. "Sounds like a you problem."

"Where's your bike now? And where did you disappear to the other day?"

I put my hands on my hips and cocked my head at him. "You're not used to struggling to keep up with a woman, are you?" It was more of a statement than a question and from the narrowing of his eyes, I could tell I had hit a nerve.

"I can keep up, brat. Just didn't know what I was up against then. I have a better idea now." His eyes fell to my lips and I felt heat rise up my neck to stain my face. He hadn't used that nickname in years and it annoyed me then, but now it felt more . . intimate. And that annoyed me even more than before.

I took a step toward my car, but he stepped closer to me and I couldn't open my door to get in the car and make the escape I really wanted to. "We have unfinished business." He said now.

"Do we?" I asked, staring at his mouth despite my best efforts not to.

"Yes, I think you know we do." He tipped my chin up until I met his gaze. "You used to annoy the piss out of me when we were kids." He reminded me and my heart started racing, but I wasn't sure if it was from anger or some foreign emotion. "Now," he said, moving close enough to breathe against my mouth. "I just want to make you scream while I'm between your legs." Before I could react, he brushed a soft kiss on my lips long enough for me to whimper and drop my hand from my car door and placed it on his side. He broke the contact and smirked down at me. "See?" He said, stroking a thumb along my lower lip. I dropped my hands to my side for a brief minute before huffing a laugh out of him. "I'm not a conquest, asshat." Just a moment ago, I was ready to find out where that light, innocent kiss would go and now I'm ready to strangle him. This man was going to be the death of me!

I opened the car door and hit him in his leg with it hard enough I was afraid I'd hurt the body panel. He didn't acknowledge the contact other than drop his hands and move away from me. I got in the car and peeled out of the driveway. I'm sure I left marks on the perfectly paved driveway, but I didn't care as I navigated the loop to leave the estate. The nerve of some assholes! I was furious. If he thought any attraction I felt could be used as leverage for whatever it is he wanted from me, he had another thing coming.

I pulled my cell phone out and dialed my father's number again and it went straight to voicemail. It was dark now and I was beyond worried and I finally let myself feel it. The fear of losing my father washed over me and the tears started to fall. I had to hurry to the house to make sure I was there in case he called or came home. He was out there somewhere, I just didn't know where.

When I got home, the house was dark and I entered the security code into the panel and disabled the alarm and then punched the code into the deadbolt pad to open the front door. I clicked on the light and the emptiness, the silence got the better of me and I started quietly sobbing as I locked up and went up stairs to shower. In the hallway at the top of the stairs, I clicked the button on the antiquated answering machine. There were two messages from Mrs. Evans, but nothing from Dad. Fear began to claw up my throat, but I squashed it down. I had to stay logical and try to get to the bottom of this. I didn't have time for the politics that Bryce and Arick had to play by. Someone somewhere had to know something.

With that thought, I gathered my keys and went back out to my car.

I knew there was a biker bar not far from the border of both pack territories, maybe I could find someone that knew something. It was a little bit of a distance, but this was my dad. I'd go to the ends of the Earth if I had to.

During the drive there, I worked through several scenarios in my head. What would I do if I found someone that knew something? How would I get them to tell me anything? Should I involve Bryce at all?

I kicked that thought out as soon as it shot through my brain. Over my dead fucking body would I call him for help.

I arrived at The Bent Star and parked away from everyone so there was no chance of me being boxed in if I had to leave in a hurry. When I walked in, I inhaled the smell of smoke, sweat and road dust. There was a line of bikes outside, it seemed like it was a busy night. Several men played pool with females hanging around them in various positions from around their neck to propped up on the wall to in one of their lap's.

Making my way to the bar, I noticed the bartender was sending a text - *rude* - before taking my order for a single beer. From there, I went to the darker corner of the bar away from the pool tables and sipped at the beer, making it seem like I was drinking it faster than I was. Matt had taught me that trick. People would surmise - incorrectly - that I was more drunk than they thought and would be more likely to relax.

I stared at the label on the brown bottle while watching the room out of the corner of my eye. It wasn't long before a biker walked up. He had dark, short hair and was wearing all black leather. The dirt on his boots told me he had been riding recently. I never understood wearing black leather to ride. It was hot and heavy and unappealing. "You look lonely, beautiful." Taking a chair out and turning it around, he sat astride it next to me. His green eyes looked me up and down. I didn't recognize him from being from our pack, but maybe he was newer to the area. He was a large man, probably a little older than Arick.

"Just have a lot on my mind," I tried to keep my tone casual.

"You can talk to me, I'm a good listener. I'm Chandler." He held his hand out for me to shake. After a moment of consideration, I slid my hand into his and he brought it to his lips. "I'm Ellie," I responded as I smiled tightly at him and brought my hand away.

"So what's on your mind, Ellie?" He motioned to a waitress that he wanted another drink and she nodded. So he was a usual, I noted.

"All kinds of things. What's the meaning of life? Why are we here?" Matt had taught me the easiest way to get information was to keep conversation light until the trust had been built. I just had to keep my new friend talking.

Chandler chuckled and appeared thoughtful. "I think the meaning of life is pleasure. By any means necessary."

I tried not to roll my eyes and shot my eyebrows up instead "By any means?"

"Well," he chuckled again. I could see why some women would think he's attractive. But I felt nothing for his looks. He was just information. "Not by force, obviously. It can be from riding, someone's warm body," he paused and raised the brown bottle the waitress sat in front of him. "Or from a good drink." He took a long drink and eyed me as the liquid moved down his throat and his Adam's apple bobbed.

Okay, I'm starting to see what women would find appealing. He was incredibly muscular and I was sure he could snap a small melon between his chest and his chin. "But Ellie," he said as he sat his beer down. "I don't think that's what's on your mind."

This time, my look of surprise was genuine. "No?"

"No. Your eyes tell me something else is going on in your life. You have many questions."

I shook my head and looked back at my bottle, fiddling with the edge of the label. "You're very astute, Chandler. Lots of questions."

He took a deep breath, looking over my face. "I'll bet this is about a man. You're confused by what you're feeling."

I frowned and it was my turn to chuckle. "I know exactly what I'm feeling. He's an ass."

Chandler threw his head back and laughed. "Well, in that case. Nothing gets you over the last one like the next one." To drive his point home, he put his hand on my wrist and I met his gaze, trying to figure out this guy's game. I felt like he knew something but he wasn't going to tell me anything without some exposed skin.

Not happening.

"Perhaps," I said now. "But there wasn't anything between us. He's just a pain in the ass."

And then, as if summoned, Bryce walked through the door.

It felt as if the air had been sucked out of the room and I was left breathless as he scanned the room until his eyes landed on me.

And narrowed.

He nodded to the bartender and walked over to me, okay *stomped* over to me and stopped at the corner of the small table, his eyes cutting between me and Chandler. It was then that Chandler stood with his hands up and walked backward away. "No harm, man."

Bryce watched him retreat and then leveled his gaze at me.

"What are you doing here?" I demanded, unable to keep the annoyance out of my tone.

"I could ask you the same thing. It's late and you weren't home." His voice was level and calm.

"So you're spying on me? Installed cameras in the woods? Or just tried to watch me from the hill again?" My voice belied a lot of emotions I didn't want to think about. I stood now and slammed my shoulder into his side as I passed him, kissing goodbye any chance of getting information about my father tonight.

I was halfway to my car before he grabbed my arm and whirled me around.

"What were you doing here, Ellie?" His voice was tense and deep. He was annoyed. Annoyed with me for not being where I was *supposed* to be. He was such an overbearing ass, I reminded myself, of course he had a box for me to be in. I wanted to kick him in his gonads but thought better of it since we were in eyeshot of other people and other potential pack members.

"I was looking for information." I jerked my arm out of his grip. "What are you doing here? Did you follow me?"

"How I got here isn't what you need to be worried about. What I'm going to do to you if you do this again is what you should be worried about." He took a step closer to drive the point home. My breath whooshed out of my lungs and I fought with my body to get it back under control before I defiantly met his gaze.

"Leave me alone, Bryce." I whirled around and headed for my car. When I got to her and started the engine, Bryce was already on his bike, putting his helmet on. I roared the engine and threw rocks behind my tires as I left the parking lot. I was speeding by the time he caught up to me. I could see his light in my rear view mirror and I pushed the accelerator harder and took the vehicle well into three digits of speed, desperate to put distance between us. The nerve of this man! I was a grown ass woman and he was treating me like a little sister that he didn't want to have to look after.

"Well then don't look after me, asshole." I muttered to myself, easily navigating the country road back to my house. I was still speeding and he was still behind me. I could have gotten information. Chandler knew something and I had wanted to explore it more, but Bryce and his big ego had messed it all up. Angry tears clouded my vision and I swiped at them in frustration. I would *not* cry right now. Not where he could potentially hear or see me.

I saw his light sway and he came up beside my window, waving his hand for me to slow down. I flipped him off and dropped a gear and took off. I knew this car well and could probably out run his bike. I cut off the main road like I had the other day on my bike and took the dirt path that would lead to my neighbor's barn and then I could creep across the grass into my driveway. But Bryce was hot on my heels and stayed with me.

Controlling the vehicles on the dirt road took some of my anger away but I was still annoyed as I pulled into my driveway and cut the engine. I heard his bike engine cut off and then he stood outside my window, his helmet still on, his gloves in fists at his side. I didn't care. I'd sit in this car until the end of time if I had to. I was not talking to him tonight.

I don't know, nor do I care how long he stood there before knocking on my car window and I just ignored him.

"Ellie!" I heard him yell through the glass and his helmet.

I crossed my arms and stuck my tongue out at him before turning to look straight ahead at my house.

He took his helmet off then and knocked on the window again. "I'm not leaving until you talk to me."

I looked to the moon and counted to ten before inching the glass down a half inch. "What?"

"I just want you to go in the house so I can make sure no one is waiting for you."

My gaze swung to him then. "Do you have reason to believe someone could be in there?" My heart started racing at the idea. I honestly hadn't thought of that.

"I don't, but I'd rather be safe. I'll go in and sweep and leave you in peace if you'll promise you'll just stay inside tonight."

I contemplated his words carefully. They made sense but I was still angry.

As if reading my mind, he offered "you can stay mad at me, I just want you safe."

No, no, *nope*. I will not be touched by anything this man says or does. Shut up, racing heart. It didn't. But as I looked at him, he shrugged. "Arick would kill me if I didn't check." And just like that, the soft and fuzzy was gone. Angry yet again, I clenched my teeth together and swung my car door, narrowly missing Bryce as I stomped to the house. I didn't care if he checked the house or not, I would do it, too. But some small part of me that I wouldn't be speaking about was grateful he was here.

I punched the code in the door and made a grand sweeping gesture. "By all means."

He went ahead of me and I started moving through the house and turning lights on. The house was still, and didn't feel like another presence was there. I was relieved for that, but let Bryce do his sweep, his helmet under his arm. I sat down on the stairs and rested my elbow on my knees and my chin on my hand while I stared at the floor.

My thoughts drifted back to the bar. How the hell had Bryce found me there?

I don't know how long I sat lost in my thoughts before he went to the door in front of my stairs. "Looks safe, keep the door locked." And he left without another word.

He closed the door and stood there, looking over his shoulder. I jumped up and locked the knob and bolt before he changed his mind. But that was what he had been waiting for and he moved off the porch to his bike. I leaned against the wall beside the door and listened until his bike was in the distance.

My emotions were wrung out and my brain couldn't make sense of any of it. So much had happened since this morning. I had just wanted to come back to Maple Springs to be at peace and get away from chaos. But the last day had been anything but peaceful.

Sighing, I left the lights on downstairs and went to my room before collapsing into bed.

Tomorrow was a new day, I told myself as my brain started to shut off for the night.

Bryce

I found myself on the hill outside her house again. The downstairs windows were illuminated. Had she gone to bed and left them on? Or was she up trying to decide her next move?

There was a war going on deep in my soul. On one hand, she showed up and all hell broke loose. On the other hand, this was *Ellie*. The bratty kid sister our trio had reluctantly cared about. She had been a harmless teenager with a crush ten years ago. There were too many coincidences for me to not think she was somehow behind this. But what alliance would she have with Santiago -the Diablo pack's Alpha- and what would either of them gain by working together? What could her father have known that would make him an asset? I couldn't believe Ellie would be dumb enough not to have someone to vouch where she was when her father disappeared, but I had given her that in spades by inviting her for a ride.

I sighed as I drew energy from the half moon. My wolf form absorbed the moonlight and I felt my weary soul ease just slightly. Ellie had felt so incredible in my arms, pressed against me. She was either a really great actress or she had enjoyed it, too. The way Megan had just warmed up to her so easily had softened my resolve toward her, but then I'd gotten the text from Sam, the bartender at the bar, that Ellie had shown up there and then that asshat was hanging on her every word.

I wanted answers, I wanted to know what was going on and she was being stubborn.

The memory of the asshole from the bar had my hackles going up, but I told myself it was because I was protective of the pack. My next move would be to find out who he was and why he'd wanted to talk to Ellie. Or had she planned to meet him there?

I had too many questions and not enough answers. Ellie was being either really great at keeping her mouth shut or being stubborn. My sudden attraction to her didn't help, either. This should be cut and dry, black and white like everything else. But her being close and making my blood boil with want didn't help anything. I sighed inwardly, life would be so easy if she'd just go back to the city. But even as the thought crossed my mind, my wolf whimpered at the thought. Whatever the hell his problem was, it wasn't mine. I was in charge and I would do everything I could to protect the pack, no matter who gave me a hard-on.

I resigned myself to get no answers and turned to head back to the pack house when movement caught my eye. My head turned, eyes searching in the moonlight. Someone was on the back porch. Someone in all black.

My heart slammed into my throat as I watched the human figure sneak up to the door and begin fiddling with the lock, looking around. He obviously hadn't seen me yet. I slipped into the cover of trees. I didn't have my cell, so shifting to human and calling for help would do no good. I would have to handle this and because it would mean protecting Ellie, it would be my pleasure to rip this asshole's throat out.

Stalking low to the ground, I made my way across the field, hiding in every shadow I possibly could. The person was kneeling by the door knob, messing with the handle of the door. Did that mean he had already conquered the number keypad?

I didn't waste much time making my way silently to the edge of the porch. I could see him in the light spilling from her windows. Ellie either didn't hear someone messing with the door or she was already upstairs asleep. I waited a heartbeat to make sure he didn't call out for anyone before I jumped and grabbed his ankle and pulled him flat on his stomach.

"Hey! What the-?" he sputtered as he rolled onto his back and that was his first -and last- mistake. I went straight to his throat, ripping it out. I heard him start to gag and cough as blood pooled on Ellie's porch. He clutched at his throat and life drained from his face slowly. I stayed in wolf form for a moment.

"What is going on out-" Ellie yanked the door open and gasped. She looked from my face, undoubtedly stained with blood to the now still body laying before her door.

"Bryce?" Her face was incredibly pale and her hand was wrapped around her own throat, like she wasn't sure if I was a crazed beast or not. I shifted and reached for her.

"Ellie-"

She gasped and stepped back. "What are *you* doing here?"

Even in danger, she was headstrong.

I met her defiant gaze as I answered, "He was trying to break in."

She gasped and took another step back, looking at the lifeless eyes now staring at the roof of the porch. "What?"

"Do you know him?" I asked, patting his body down for identification of some kind. He didn't appear very tall and was bald. He'd been wearing all black, which means he knew he was to break in, which erased any question if Ellie was expecting him or not.

I looked up at her now, having turned nothing up on our dead friend.

Her face was puffy from sleep and her silver hair was mused. She was still wearing the clothes she'd had on and that damn low neck on her shirt was even lower now. Her big, round eyes looked at me and she blinked. "No, I haven't seen him before. What do you mean he was trying to break in?" She knelt to examine the door handle. "Bastard scratched my door knob." she muttered as she rubbed at it. I glanced at his hand, he'd been wearing gloves so as not to leave any evidence. My blood ran cold as I imagined what he'd planned for Ellie. Kill her? Kidnap her? Was she involved in the equation at all? Or were they looking for something in the house that the Doctor was hiding?

"Um," she said now, looking me over from head to toe, pausing for a *really* long time half way. "You don't have any clothes on."

I shrugged and made no move to cover myself. "I was out patrolling. Picked up a scent and followed it." I was *not* going to tell her I'd been walking around her back yard like a stalker.

She cleared her throat and finally looked away. "Do you want to call someone?"

A small part of me swelled with pride before I could push it down; she wasn't fragile and freaking out there was a dead body on her porch. Death and blood was part of our lives as shifters, especially if there is tension between packs. Which something told me was about to happen now.

"That would be nice, thank you." I might be naked, but I could still have manners.

She stepped aside and let me in but stepped out on the porch and looked around into the night.

"He was alone," I called over my shoulder as I picked up the phone in the kitchen. I dialed the pack house security and told them to get a few guys to Ellie's -the Doctor's- house for clean up. Then my next call was to Arick to bring him up to speed. He'd obviously been asleep, but woke up as soon as I explained what had transpired.

"What the fuck?" I heard the covers rustle off of him as he was moving to get dressed. "I'll be right there. Keep Ellie calm." I looked at her now, moving around the kitchen starting a pot of coffee while a dead man lay in the threshold of her kitchen door, blood soaking through the wood.

"I think it'll be okay on that front." I muttered.

Arick disconnected the call and I leaned against the wall, watching Ellie as she moved around the kitchen.

"I didn't have anything to do with him being here, if that's what you're thinking." She said without looking at me. The coffee maker started dripping and she just stood looking out the window over the sink. "This has been such a fucked up day." She sighed and rubbed her eyes.

"I've got some guys coming to take care of it. We'll get the wood on the porch cleaned and repainted, too."

She whirled around then, her eyes wild. "You think *that's* what I'm worried about? How about you thinking I'm behind every bad thing that's happened in the last twenty four hours? How about you're spying on me and following me?"

I didn't really have an answer for that, she had me. Her father had disappeared, we had asked her to help a young woman get ready for her shift, I had bullied her at the bar and then I killed someone that had been about to break into her home. She'd had a really shitty day.

"You're right. I'm sorry."

She snorted and turned around again.

There was a knock at the front door, saving me from having to figure out the next thing to say. As she pushed past me, I noticed how careful she was to keep her eyes anywhere but on me. But I smirked. She was into what she saw.

"He's back there." I heard her say and pictured her pointing past the stairs into the kitchen.

The next few hours were a blur. Damon had brought me clothes, and the body was loaded into a truck they had lined with plastic. Jason informed me that they had found the guy's car down the road and they would investigate who he was and who had sent him and handle it.

I had every bit of faith in their abilities, but I wanted to stay close to this one. "I want every update as it becomes available." I said, looking out into the night. I'd also like shit to start making sense, but kept that to myself. Jason nodded grimly at my expectation and Damon stifled a groan. It was going to be a lot of work, but they understood what was at risk.

"What about security here? In case someone else is sent?" Jason asked now, eyeing the house behind me.

I'd already been playing with that idea. We couldn't afford the man power to have someone posted and Ellie would likely throw a fit if I tried. "Just add the property to the patrols. If anyone picks up anything or she leaves, I want to know about it."

Jason and Damon left without another word and I turned to find Ellie standing at the top of the five steps up to the wrap around porch on the front of the house. At some point in the chaos, she had changed clothes, wearing an oversize T-shirt off one shoulder and *short* shorts. Her hair was falling around her shoulders, the bare skin of her left shoulder playing peekaboo in the soft breeze. My mouth was going dry, even seeing the angry look on her face. Her arms were crossed, pushing her breasts up and her stance was wide with a *don't fuck with me* vibe that had me weak in the knees.

"If I leave my home?" She asked. Before I could respond, she uncrossed her arms and stomped down to me. "Listen to me, you pigheaded *asshole.*" The stress on the word was punctuated by her poking my chest through my shirt. "I am loyal to this pack. I went to the city ten years ago because my *brother* and *your best friend* had died. You were in no position to get me through that." She punctuated her words more by poking my chest. "Now" poke "I'm" poke "back" poke "and you can't" poke "handle" poke "that I'm not some easy lay. I suggest you get out of my life, way or whatever the

~ 76 ~

fuck you want to call it and go find out why a neighboring pack wants to take my father." Poke, poke, poke.

I grasped her fist in mine and yanked her close. She yelped as she fell against me, her eyes locking with mine.

"I don't take orders from brats, first of all. Second, None of this happened until *you*" my turn to poke her chest. "Came back. Now everything is being shipped to Hell in an express envelope and you're out meeting other pack scouts in strange bars." Remembering the last part had me pissed off. I pushed her away from me and ignored my wolf yapping for her to come back. "I can tolerate a lot of things, Ellie. But I will not, *cannot* tolerate a traitor."

She gasped and I felt bad for a split second until her hand came across my face, disgust twisting her features. Her eyes told me that she regretted it, but her recoiling into herself told me she was scared. I took a step toward her and she took off running up the stairs, but I was hot on her heels. She tried to slam the door in my face, but I was able to wedge myself between it and the jam and force it open. Ellie stumbled backward, but I was there to catch her before she fell to the floor. I walked her back to the wall of the hallway leading to the kitchen. Grabbing her ample ass, I pushed her up the wall until she was eye level with me. I heard her swift gasp as her eyes searched mine before falling to my mouth, which I felt becoming a snarl.

"I'm not upset that you're not an easy lay, either." I said, my face still throbbing from her slap. Who the hell taught her to hit like that? Holding her securely against the wall with my torso, I cupped her neck, looking at her mouth and knowing it was right there for me to take. To take whatever I wanted, she wouldn't resist me.

"But keep testing me, and I'll make sure you get what you've been craving — rough, and without mercy until I break that bratty attitude of yours." I released her and stepped away before I did something I couldn't stop or take back. Leaving her against the wall shaking, I walked out the door into the waning night.

Chapter Five

Ellie

My heart was racing and my knees were trembling. I couldn't believe I had slapped him and regretted letting my anger get the best of me. I closed my eyes and let my head thud against the wall, unwilling to let myself watch Bryce walk out the door. But the moment my eyes closed, Bryce's muscular body flashed through my mind like a porno. Why did he have to have so much muscle? And why did I have to notice? Even now my fingers pulled at me to trace those muscles in my mind, trying to figure out which ones were erogenous. I wanted to trace the pack insignia on his pec with my tongue. With a grunt, I pushed off the wall, balling my hands into fists. This had to be a dream, right? I would just wake up and I'd be in my boring bedroom, leading my boring life, waiting for some boring things to do. Right? There was no way I had been kissed by my childhood crush, had my house almost broken into, a dead body-

I stopped myself there and glanced down the hallway to the kitchen. From where I stood, I could see the back door was closed, but the stain on the linoleum was visible. Highly visible. Bryce had said the pack would handle it, but I hadn't missed the way he had looked at me. I'm sure he'd been waiting for me to wither and melt like someone that had never seen a body before. In my work in the city, I'd seen more than my fair share of people that had crossed the line and not lived to tell the tale. I wasn't exactly used to it, just desensitized. If you stay out of places you don't belong, you get to keep breathing. Some part of me was grateful Bryce had been stalking about my yard and had seen someone trying to get in. A shudder moved through me at the thought of what would have happened if he hadn't been there. I had been asleep, completely unaware of everything going on around me. I hadn't heard anything until I heard Bryce's growl and the snarl as he'd gotten the man on his back.

I went to the door and opened it, looking at the blood still on the porch. Damn him, I thought as I slammed the door shut again. If he had left him alive, we- *I* -could have gotten some answers. Now I was still Bryce's top suspect and I was no closer to finding out where my father was. I didn't want to think about what had happened to my father, I knew he was still out there and alive. I just had no idea where. I poured myself a cup of coffee and sipped at it while watching the sun come up over the field. Somewhere, there were pack members watching my land, waiting for me to do something.

Well, they could stay there until hell froze over. I was going to find answers. Somewhere in this house is what the dead man had wanted. That meant I had a lot more answers than I thought I did. I just had to think about where it could be and start there.

A knock at the front door drew me from my thoughts and I yelped in surprise. I'm going to need some sleep soon or I'm not going to be good for anything. Moving cautiously down the hallway,

I checked the window on the door and saw Arick there and opened the door with a wide sweep.

"Good . . . morning? I have no idea what time it is." I said as I led him to the kitchen without another word. I could feel him looking around the house as he followed me, no doubt absorbed in memories like I was when I first got home from the city.

"They didn't get into the house?" I rolled my eyes at his question. Straight down to business.

"No, Bryce was there before he could breach the door. He was working on the lock, I think."

Arick opened the kitchen door and glanced down at the blood everywhere. Damn, I hadn't realized it was on the door, too. I'd have to clean it before it drew bugs.

"You don't know who he was?" His question hung in the air as he closed the door again.

"No, Bryce already interrogated me about it. I don't know anything, other than he was trying to get into the house." I couldn't keep the annoyance out of my voice as I fixed Arick a cup of coffee. I remembered he took it black, so I handed it over to him and sat at the table. My eyes felt heavy and I just wanted everyone to leave me alone. But there wasn't a chance of that happening.

Arick sat down and eyed me as he sipped the hot coffee, then sat the cup down. He leveled a look at me and I only looked at him over the edge of my cup. "Do you feel safe here? We have cabins you would be safer at." He offered.

I slammed my coffee down, sloshing it onto the table. "I'm not leaving my home. My father could be home at any minute and I don't want him to think I got taken, too."

Arick held his hands up in defense before picking his coffee back up. "Okay, I'm not arguing. Just making an offer."

I sighed and rested my face in my hands, elbows on the table. "I know, I'm sorry. It's been a really long day. Bryce thinks I'm behind everything bad in the universe and my father is missing. I could use a friend and not an enemy."

Arick nodded slowly and sipped from his cup. "I get it. Bryce is just trying to look out for the pack."

"He's being an ass about it."

Arick chuckled and shook his head. "You haven't changed a bit."

I opened my mouth to argue but I was tired and the slight humor I saw in Arick's eyes stopped me. We had been a gang, whether the boys had wanted me there or not. It had been a good time in my life, until it wasn't. The thought passed through my brain to share with Arick that whatever my uninvited guest had wanted was still somewhere in the house and I was going to find it. But I thought better of it. The last thing I needed was an Alpha and his Beta tearing my house apart. No, I would find what it was and then figure out how to bargain for my father back.

Arick looked over his shoulder at the door again, a single brow going up. I noticed not for the first time in my life that Arick was incredibly handsome. His dirty blond hair was pulled back in a ponytail today and his tattoos went down his arms to his fingers where a ring adorned almost all of his fingers. But he had never drawn my attention like Bryce had. "I wonder," Arick said now. "What that person was after. And if he knew you were here."

I took too big of a swallow of hot coffee, which made my eyes tear up as it burned down my throat. "Of course he knew," I choked out. "My car is outside."

Arick's alert eyes cut to me and I struggled to look innocent. Wait, I was innocent, I just had an inkling of what my next move was and didn't feel like sharing. Still drilling holes into me with his eyes, he changed the subject. "Megan will be home all day if you just want to come see her and relax for a bit."

I cleared my throat and looked away, letting myself feel tired and hoping it came through my face. "I appreciate it. I'm going to get some sleep and try to start the day over later."

Arick thankfully took the hint. "Thanks for the coffee. I hope to see you later this afternoon, then." I heard the front door open and close and then an engine start and roll away.

I didn't know where Bryce was, so I was going to stay put. I didn't him charging at me over seeing Megan again. Putting my coffee on the table, I moved to the edge of the hallway. Without my father here, the house was silent. Every gust of wind, every creak in the floor boards seemed to echo in my head. I was exhausted, my muscles starting to ache from the stress but I knew the stillness wouldn't let me rest. Not while this house held answers for me. With that thought, determination set in my chest and I found myself moving to my father's study.

He had never been very apt at keeping records, but there had to be something that showed where he had been yesterday. And the day before that.

I was willing to place money on the fact he had heard something somewhere, but I had to find patient records, trip logs, *something* to show his whereabouts for the week.

Time was ticking away and I was going to get my answers. I was determined.

~*~

I don't know how long I scoured every file, letter, bill or paper I could find. But the sun was high in the sky by the time I stretched in my father's desk chair. My vertebrae popped several times, pulling a sigh of relief from me. My face scrunched as I surveyed the office. It wasn't a disaster, but you could tell I had gone through *everything*.

My search hadn't turned up his patient log, notes or his backup prescription pad, which would normally be in the locked drawer. Not only was the drawer not locked, but the pads were missing. If there was something here, I was confident that someone outside of my dad's life wouldn't be able to find it either.

A sad sigh slipped past my lips as I slumped against the top of the desk, my head in my hands. We had talked several times every week over the last ten years, until I'd had to start skirting around what exactly I was up to in the city. Then it was just me pressing him about his eating habits, making sure he was taking care of himself and checking in to make sure he was still coming to the city for Christmas and other holidays. Sadness continued to wash over me and I let myself wallow in it. I hadn't been the doting daughter he'd needed. His wife had run off and his son had died, then I'd taken off to the city with my aunt to avoid confronting my own feelings. He had been left alone to deal with things on his own. I resolved there that if, *when* I found him, that would change.

The shrill of the phone on the desk brought me back to the present with a start. It hadn't rung all day and I began to wonder who knew he was missing?

I cleared my throat as I picked up the receiver. "Hello?"

"Ellie? It's Helena." I recognized the voice as one of my dad's oldest friends. Actually, she had been friends with his parents. I hadn't seen her since I was a *little* little kid. I was surprised she recognized me or even remembered who I was.

"Oh, hi." I paused briefly. "Dad isn't here right now. Do you want me to take a message?"

There was a long pause that had my heart racing. All the hair on my arms stood on end. "Helena? Are you okay?" My voice sounded breathless.

"It's Alyssa. Harry was supposed to see her yesterday but I haven't heard a thing from her and she's not answering her phone either. I'm really worried."

A *zing* went up my spine and I forced myself to remain calm. Alyssa was Helena's granddaughter. I didn't know her well, she was a few years my senior. I remembered her as reclusive and a loner. Her best friend had been her grandmother in her youth. If Helena hadn't heard from her, something was amiss. "I can run over and check on her. Do you know what dad saw her for?"

Helena cleared her throat and mumbled to herself for a moment. "She only told me she wasn't feeling well. I would go check on her myself, but I don't get around so good anymore, Ellie."

I took a quiet deep breath. "It's not a problem, I'll go check on her and see if there's anything I can do."

"Thank you, Ellie. I'm glad you're home."

Helena gave me directions to Alyssa's house and we disconnected the call with my promise I'd call her back with my findings. My fatigue evaporated as I headed to the door. This could tell me a lot about what happened yesterday leading up to dad's disappearance. The address that Helena gave me was at the edge of our territory near where the grounds were supposed to be developed. A quick survey of the front told me that the dogs were out on patrols and not near me. I made my way to my car, now dusty as hell from the drive last night and turned it around to head to the edge of town.

My mind was racing a million miles a minute with questions to ask to get the most information. She had to have been one of the last people to talk to him. Was he acting weird? Had he taken any phone calls while there? Did he mention anything about the rest of his day?

When I got to the small rancher, everything was incredibly still. Eerily so and the the hair on my neck stood up *again*. But for a different reason. The stillness wasn't passing the vibe check in any sense of the words.

I went up to the steps and knocked on the door. "Alyssa? It's Ellie, Dr. Savoy's daughter." Before I could call again, I heard the unmistakable sound of Bryce's bike rolling up to my car. I hung my head down and refused to look at him for several minutes. I don't know how long I stood there with the sun on my back while he just sat astride his bike, but I finally chanced a peek at him. He was dressed in all black and looked dangerous as hell. Still astride his bike, his gloved hands rested on his thighs as he just sat staring at me. Anger was on the rise as I stomped down the front steps.

"What are you doing here?" I tried to put even more agitation in my tone, hoping he realized how annoyed I was with him.

"I could ask you the same thing, sweetheart." His voice was muffled through his helmet and all I could see in his visor was my reflection. The deep timbre of his voice did things to my girly parts I didn't want to talk about. Poking his chest again, I let my full on agitation grow. "I'm here checking on one of dad's patients. Which is none of *your* business."

He pulled his helmet off then and smirked at me. Oh how I would love to smack that smirk off his face. "It's pack business. I'll come with you."

I released a frustrated groan. "What can I say to get you to change your mind?"

"Oh Bryce," He said, rolling his eyes with a high pitch mocking voice. "Take me home on your bike and fuck my attitude out of me." Leveling another look at me, his smirk returned. "Anything short of that and I'm not leaving until you do."

I turned on my heel, grinding my teeth because I was not willing to give into his childishness. After I marched back up the steps to the house, I tried knocking again. The door, well the entire house, was really run down, I noticed. If Bryce cared so damn much, he should be helping the pack keep a roof over their heads.

"Alyssa?" I knocked harder. "It's Ellie!"

"Did you try the knob or the back?" Bryce asked, no hint of sarcasm or arrogance this time. My quick glance at his face showed he was growing concerned, too. Maybe she wasn't home?

At the first twist of the knob, the door swung open and I was greeted with a horrific smell. Bryce grabbed my shoulders and turned me back down the steps. "Nope, not this time." He said, leading me to the hood of my car as my stomach heaved at the smell. I lost my coffee on the ground in front of my car as he pulled his cell phone out and hit two buttons.

"Call Vince. We've got a dead person out by the grounds."

Chapter Six

Ellie

"You were here, why exactly, Miss Savoy?"

"I told you, Sheriff. Her grandmother Helena called me and asked if I could check on her."

It was almost dark now, the county crime scene van had removed the body of a badly decomposed Alyssa several hours ago and a team was combing the house. Vince Dodds was a shifter like us and could keep our territories at peace for the most part. I hadn't thought to call him when Dad's truck was found and I wasn't sure if he even knew I hadn't seen my dad in over twenty-four hours.

I saw Bryce and Arick by the house, speaking to each other in hushed tones. They would have their hands full keeping this under wraps from humans in the area. But I couldn't bring myself to care, I had come here to try to get some answers and now I had even more questions. Did my dad even see Alyssa yesterday? How could he if she was that badly decomposed? It had smelled like she had been dead for a really long time. I didn't have any patient records on when she would have called Dad to come see her and all Helena knew was that Alyssa had asked for help yesterday.

As if sensing my eyes on him, Bryce's gaze turned to meet mine. No doubt he was putting together how I was returning to the scene of my own crime and it was a *damned good thing* that he had followed me here to catch me. But as I searched his eyes, even from this distance I almost saw . . . sympathy? Hell, no. Narrowing my gaze, I broke the contact first. There was no way in hell I'd let him feel sorry for me.

"I promised Helena I'd call her," I said lamely. There was no comparing my feelings with what Helena would be feeling when she found out. Vince cleared his throat. I have a deputy on the way over there now. I nodded and rubbed my shoulder absently. I wasn't sure what I was feeling right now but I didn't want to be here another minute. "Do you need me anymore, Sheriff? It's been a long day."

Vince looked up from his notepad and his expression softened. "That's fine. Don't leave town and stay near your phone in case I have more questions."

With a small sign of relief, I got in my car without a word to Arick or Bryce. As I backed away from the house, the yard and the Alpha and Beta, I saw both of them watching me. Damn them both, I didn't care. I had no answers and my father was still gone. Tears welled in my eyes as I took my time getting home.

The house was dark and guilt clawed at me again for not knowing my father's life better than I did. Once I was inside, I did a quick sweep through the house to make sure I was alone. But as I passed Dad's room, I saw it just as it had been for a few days and I couldn't stop the tears this time. He was out there in the world somewhere, undoubtedly hurt and alone. Visions flashed in my mind of him tied up, being punched until bloody. Pistol whipped and maybe even shot for information. I was no stranger to how people like this operated. The visions kept dancing in my head and fear clawed at my throat and ate away at my sanity until I was down the stairs, through the kitchen and on the back porch. I locked up and took a breath as tears streamed down my face. Before I realized what I was doing, I dissolved into my pain and felt the fur come out of my skin, my bones clicked and crunched as I became my wolf. The half-moon was dancing with clouds in the sky as I ran across the back field toward the woods where my father was last traced. I was going to find answers, Grayson and his diplomacy be damned. Through the deep cover of night, I ran through the trees, reveling in the feel of the leaves and twigs under my paws, feeling a sense of belonging that I hadn't felt in a long time. I sensed and smelled other wolves in the area the closer I got to the breach in the woods. I remembered that Bryce had ordered increased patrols so I didn't let it stop me as the wind whipped past my ears and I moved closer to the break in the woods where a patch of moonlight spilled onto the high grass. My breath left my lung as I jumped over a fallen tree and I was airborne. I felt so right, so at ease, so free.

I caught my father's scent, though faint. My nose to the ground, I sorted the smells of the Earth and grass and traced his scent to where we had stood with his truck. I could still see the impressions of the truck tires. I still had my nose to the ground, desperate to find some trace of my father. I found Bryce's instead and my senses wouldn't let me leave it alone. It filled my nose and made my head swim. Dammit, this was infuriating even while intoxicating. I forced myself to move away from where he had stood, where we had stood face to face as I dared him to do something, though I didn't know what.

But around the truck, I found no other scents. Only Damon's, Bryce's and mine. How was that possible if my father had been here and left the truck? I looked over the field, eyeing the Navarro domain. There were wolves on the other side. But they weren't ours. They were Diablo pack wolves. Which meant this was escalating and at the core was my father.

I cautiously moved toward the lines and waited for one of the wolves to approach me, staying on our side.

"What do you want?" the Gray wolf asked, his head low. He was ready to charge, but then he caught my scent and knew I was female.

"What do you know of the doctor coming onto your land?" I asked cautiously. One of the other wolves pacing back and forth stopped and looked to his leader.

They exchanged a glance. "Your alpha already contacted us. We're upping our patrols. You'd do well to stay away from the lines." The gray wolf finally answered.

"Please! He's my father, I just want to know he's okay." I pleaded, knowing this wolf knew something.

"Ellie!" The deep voice invaded my mind and I wanted to scream. He couldn't possibly be everywhere at once, yet somehow he always seemed to be there every time I turned around.

"They know something, Bryce." I answered him with my head low, ready to charge the gray wolf.

"Leave." Was all he said to me as he approached and stood just in front of me, facing the other pack.

Angry, but unable to defy the Beta in front of another pack, I took off running. I was so angry as I raced through the woods, desperate to get away from Bryce, away from the other pack, away from all the scents. This had been a mistake; I should have known better. I reached my porch in record time and changed back to human, pulling my shirt over my head. Still trembling and fighting angry tears, I struggled with the number pad on the door. I finally cried out, nearly screaming as I beat on the door, frustrated with everything.

Suddenly, I was pulled to a naked chest and strong arms wrapped my shoulders and I was powerless to resist. I just leaned into it and sobbed until I didn't have anything left to feel, I was just raw and feeling like a knife had been ripped down my chest, revealing a gaping wound ten years old. When the sobs stopped, I stilled. It was then that I realized I was in a T-shirt on my porch being held by a very naked Bryce. How many times had I imagined this very thing? The irony wasn't lost on me and I looked up at his face now, the shadows from the clouds moving around us as he brushed the tears from my cheeks.

I was staring at his lips when his thumb moved to trace my own lips and suddenly I didn't care what tomorrow would bring. A need deep in my chest was burning white hot fire and only Bryce could put it out. "Bryce," I sounded breathless to my own ears. He closed his eyes and took a deep breath, but his body was reacting to being near me.

In the next moment, his mouth was on mine. He tasted like the woods and smelled of the earth. It was drowning my senses and I knew I was already wet for him, like I was in heat. I wrapped my arms around his neck and he lifted my ass in his large hands until my legs hooked around his waist and he slammed me into the wall next to the door. His hard-on pushed against me, answering my question if this was going to happen or not. Yes, this was happening and it felt delicious. Like an itch that had been ignored for a long time and it was finally going to get scratched. I moaned as he kissed his way down my neck before ripping my shirt open with his teeth and one hand. Once my breasts were free, he kissed his way to one nipple while holding the other one against his palm. I cried out and arched against him from the wall, wanting him so bad I thought I was going to combust from the heat between my legs. My hands clenched at his hair to keep him from stopping. I wiggled my hips against him, trying to get him in, but he stopped sucking and biting my nipple long enough to chuckle. "Easy, brat. I've got plans for you."

My body began trembling at his words but I couldn't find the words to answer him, I could only moan. Kissing my lips again, he forced his tongue into my mouth and I accepted it, wanting to take every part of him in me. It was a delicious torment he was wracking on me and I didn't want it to ever end.

He moved us closer to the door. "Put in the code." He said against my mouth. Helpless, I did what he told me to do as he nibbled the side of my neck. I was so wet I felt it running on my thigh and I had to be heavy for him, but he didn't protest or try to put me down as he carried me inside and kicked the door shut. He put me down on the floor in the kitchen and I nearly cried out, afraid it was over. Instead, he bent and swept me into the air and kissed me again, navigating my house in the dark as he walked up stairs, carrying me to my room. He laid me gently on my bed and I moved to the far side so he could get in the bed. But instead, he grabbed my ankle and turned me around so my legs were on either side of his hips and began nibbling on my neck again before biting me hard enough to leave a mark and the feeling so delicious I arched against him, wanting more. Wanting him.

He kissed his way down my chest, lifting my breasts with his hands and thumbing the nipples as he kissed his way down to my navel. I felt him pause at my belly ring and he chuckled. "That is incredibly sexy." He said as his hands came to lift my knees up and tilt my body toward his. I felt a single finger touch me and I cried out as I arched off the bed. "Easy, brat. We're just getting started." He then grasped both of my ass cheeks in his hands as he tipped me up and I froze in anticipation. He pulled me closer and I felt his tongue separate me and I arched against his face, digging my heels into the bed beneath me. "Bryce!"

He moaned against me, which only deepened the contact. "Yes, that's it. Scream my name." He sucked my clit between his teeth and nibbled so gently I was ready to die. But I needed deeper contact, needed him inside me. "Please." I begged as he continued to torment me.

"Not yet," he said and then his tongue swept the length of me, but not deep enough.

"Bryce!"

"You're driving me crazy, brat. You taste so good." He moaned against me as he drank more of me, played with my clit while his hands roughly grasped my ass. I was sure I was bruising but it felt so right. Like I was being marked as his.

"Bryce, please. . ." I begged more. I needed this to end or I was going to lose my mind. There was so much pleasure, so much pressure between my legs, but it wasn't enough. It wasn't enough of him.

"Tell me what you want," he commanded softly, lazily licking my slit.

"I need your cock, Bryce. Please." I had no shame, I begged him until I was ready to sob his name.

"I don't think you want it bad enough." He said against me before flicking my clit with his tongue. I made a sound I wasn't sure what it was, somewhere between a cry and a moan. He released one side of my ass and I felt his fingers move from the sensitive hole that tightened at his touch. He stopped licking my clit to watch his hand move around my puckered hole. "You're so wet, it would be so easy to take you right now.."

I moaned and pushed against his fingers, insane with want and need I would let him do anything to me at that point. With a slow motion, he finally moved to my pussy and I felt my breath catch and hold in my throat, waiting for his next move. He followed the same path his tongue had, moving around my clit and down again, teasing at fucking me without actually entering me. My head fell back, my chest was heaving and I felt the bed wet beneath my ass from his teasing me. When I thought I was going to die from want, he finally sunk a single finger into my pussy and I immediately clenched around it. He was still watching me and groaned as he watched the single finger begin to fuck my pussy.

"Fuck, brat. You're so wet."

I could only groan and move to meet his finger. It still wasn't enough. "Bryce," I sobbed, needing more and he knew it.

"What do you need? Tell me."

"Fuck me." I begged, arching against his single finger.

"You haven't earned that. Do you want to cum?"

My hand clenched the blanket under me and I arched against him again. "Please."

"Please, what?" He asked now, slowing his finger down.

"Please let me cum. Please, Bryce."

"Oh, fuck I love when you beg." His head went back between my legs and now two fingers were in me, working me hard while he sucked on my clit. I could feel myself racing up a hill toward that crest and I moved against his face and his fingers and when I was almost there, he sunk another finger in and that was it.

I felt like I was flying apart, reassembling against his face and flying apart again into a million pieces.

He moaned against my clit. "That was beautiful." His voice was hoarse. "Give me more."

And he kept moving the three fingers inside my pussy as his tongue circled my clit. I was sure that I had nothing left, but it was only a few strokes of those clever fingers before I was racing up that hill again. I grabbed his head and held him still as I came again, this time wave after wave of pleasure washing over the million pieces he had shattered me into.

Quickly, he stood again and was then on top of me, entering me before I could do anything. I cried out and arched into him. I smelled my juice on his face and it only drove me crazy and I tried to move against him, to deepen the contact, still spasming from the last orgasm but somehow desperate for more. "That's it. Brat. Want it." He drove deep then, pulling me close to his chest while he was braced on his elbows. Then he was taking me fast and I could only hold on as his thrusts grew rapid and I got so close again.

When I thought I would die from the pleasure, I felt myself come apart in his arms and milked him for everything he could give me. "Oh fuck, brat. Fuck." He tensed above me, and I felt his cum deep inside me and I tilted my hips to take more of him, milk all of it out of him until he was as satiated as I was. As I came back to my senses, I felt him smooth my hair from my face and I looked at him then. I expected to see anger, disgust, frustration. But instead, there was a tenderness as he watched me. "Did I hurt you?" He asked now.

I let out a little laugh. "Not at all." I kissed under his chin and held him close for a minute, savoring the feeling of him being this close. He was still in me, but I felt his cum running down my leg to the bed below. "We should shower." I said lamely. He stood and offered me his hand, unashamed to be in my bedroom, naked and evidence of what we had just done all over him. I thought he would release my hand once I stood, but instead he pulled me close and kissed me as he walked me backward toward the shower. I felt something blooming in my chest I didn't dare name as he leaned past me to start the water to warm it up and then kiss his way down my neck to my shoulder, where he nipped at my tattoo. He raised his head and traced the lines with his finger. "Beautiful." He said, and then looked into my eyes. My tattoo was our pack's insignia. I had gotten it to keep myself rooted to the pack, even though I wasn't living here. The one on his bicep was much larger, but the same. I had been there with him when he'd gotten it. I smiled at him and then turned to step into the shower, but he grasped my wrist.

"I didn't say you could do that." He said and I thought he was teasing, but when I looked into his eyes, I saw he was serious.

I arched a brow at him. "I don't remember asking."

A laugh rumbled up in his chest and danced around my head. "Keep on, I'll have to punish you."

Despite what we'd just done, I felt my body reacting at his words and I could only gape at him. To answer my unspoken question, he slapped my ass. Hard. And I felt myself get even wetter and my nipples harden. This drew his gaze and he smirked at me. "That's better."

He pulled the shower door open and pushed me inside at the small of my back and I didn't know what my next move was going to be. I was reacting to this side of Bryce in a way that had me extremely confused. I hadn't known what this side of him would be like, but I had never expected him to be so commanding. So dominating.

While I stood by like a dummy, he took a washcloth and soap and began washing me, ridding my body of all the evidence of what we had done. But as his hand moved over my body, I was beginning to want him again. He took extra time to wash my breasts, carefully massaging each of them and running his thumb over my nipples and from the way he watched his hands, he knew what he was doing. Then his hands were on my ass, between my legs and in every crevice until I was straining against his hand as he washed me.

"Want more, brat?" He asked, enjoying my torment a bit too much.

I nodded because I couldn't get my voice to work in that moment as hunger clawed at my body. Hunger for him. He took down the shower head and rinsed all the soap off my skin, following the shower head with his hand, which only drove me wilder.

"Bryce . . . " I whispered.

He dropped the shower head and pushed me against the wall, his hand between my legs, caressing my clit as I squirmed, trying to deepen the contact.

"Yes," he said as he kissed me again. I could only hold onto his shoulders as his finger moved in and out of me in a delicious rhythm that had me panting. I squirmed against him more and he slid another finger inside me and I threw my head back and cried out. "Yes, like that." He growled in my ear and I felt another orgasm begin lower in my belly and rip through me and this time I did scream until I was sure the glass would break. "That's it, I love hearing your screams while you squeeze my fingers." I could only whimper as his fingers kept going and I felt another orgasm building. I was tense, clutching at his shoulders. But he already knew. He didn't stop, just kept the same rhythm until it finally broke and I screamed until my throat was sore. Then all I could do was go limp against the shower wall. He held me there while he grabbed the shower head and finished washing himself off, careful not to torment me anymore before picking me up again and carrying me to the bed where he laid us down, throwing the wet blanket from earlier on the floor.

He laid me down and we both got under the covers. It vaguely occurred to me that he was sleeping with me, but I was so weak I didn't care as he gathered me to his chest and absently rubbed my shoulder and I fell asleep breathing in his scent, my scent.

Our scent.

Chapter Seven

Bryce

I watched her sleeping against my side. I had been awake awhile, for a mix of reasons. One, half-listening in case those Navarro wolves followed us into our territory. Two, experiencing Ellie had me shaken to my core. She smelled and tasted unlike any other woman I'd ever had. It was intoxicating and now I had to decide next steps. She wasn't my mate, so would we continue as lovers? She was a childhood friend, would we go back to just being friends? My arm unconsciously tightened around her shoulders as I thought of being around her and not touching her, tasting her again. I guess I knew which way I'd rather things go. But I also couldn't ignore the big ass elephant, either. Her father was missing, a pack member was dead and we had way too many questions with no answers.

One of the patrols had texted me yesterday that Ellie had left the house and I'd been on my bike quick. I'd picked up her trail at a crossroad and followed her from a distance. She had been so lost in whatever she'd been thinking she didn't even notice I was tailing her. The determination I'd seen in trying to run me off so she could investigate on her own had riled me up at the same time it turned me on. Ellie was a force to be reckoned with, and I'd chase the little storm wherever she'd go, I realized. With an inward sigh, I accepted she was as desperate for answers as I was. I didn't think she had anything to do with the disappearance of her father or Alyssa's murder. And it had been murder. Vince had said her throat had been torn out and the house tossed like someone had been looking for something. I felt like the answer was staring me in the face but I couldn't put my finger on it all.

Beside me, Ellie took a deep breath and stretched against me and I felt her large tits rub against my skin and I felt like pinning her down again and not leaving this bed for the rest of the day. Hell, the rest of the year. But there was an entire world out there, and her missing father was out there somewhere in it. Staying wasn't an option right now.

I felt her freeze and tense, one eye opening and scanning the room before resting on me. "Oh, shit." She muttered, scooting as far from my side as she could and sitting up on her elbows, pulling the sheet over her chest like I hadn't seen it before. She was blinking rapidly, now looking all over the room. Anywhere but at me. She cleared her throat and peered at me from below her lashes. "What time is it?" She asked quietly, now still as death.

"Just after 7," I responded, rolling to my side and propping myself up on my elbow to look at her. My inner asshole wanted to play with her, push her limits even while I saw her scrambling to put walls back up that had crumbled to the ground last night after the hopelessness of trying to locate her father. She sat up then, still holding the sheet but holding it with her elbows while she scrubbed at her face. I could see all of her back, down to that perfect ass. I now saw the tattoo between her shoulder blades, two wolves. A black and a white one arranged in a yin and yang.

I knew she was the white wolf, a pure wolf with blue eyes, but as far as I knew I was the only all black wolf she knew. Unless it was for Matt. The thought tightened my chest and I wanted to put a fist through the wall.

"Listen-" She started, turning to me and interrupting my thoughts. "Last night was-"

"Incredible?" I asked smugly with a smirk. I had no doubt in my mind she had enjoyed every moment of what I had done to her body.

She released a frustrating sigh. "I'm not dissing quality here."

I yawned lazily now, determined to piss her off for reasons beyond me. "Better not. That was some of my best work." I stretched my arms above my head and laid back on her pillows with my hands behind my head, forcing a calm I didn't really feel. But I didn't miss how she eye-fucked me, looking me over from head to just below my abs where the sheet laid lazily. And then my body started reacting to her gaze.

She cleared her throat and cut her gaze away quickly. "That's not what I was about to say."

"Okay, what were you about to say?" I felt tense, knowing what she was trying to do.

"We can't do it again." She blurted out. "It crossed the line of friendship and Arick would probably kill us both."

I considered her words for a minute. Some part of me had known she would try to push me back to friendzone. But after last night, she wasn't just some one-night stand. This was different. I couldn't just walk away and pretend it didn't matter. That I didn't want more.

"Okay." Was all I said.

Her eyes cut to mine quickly. "So you agree?" I couldn't tell if her eyes held surprise or disappointment, but her tone was straight shock.

I sat up, moving closer to her. "I didn't say that, brat." Her face turned a bright red, remembering what that term means now, how that dynamic had shifted from annoyed brother's friend to lovers. "I'll just have to convince you we're good together. Then we can do that lots of times and I can show you more of the good stuff." I kissed her shoulder and got out of bed. I'd have to shift to wolf to get to the pack house because I didn't have clothes here, but I wasn't in a hurry to rush off. To face the world outside this new place I'd found with Ellie.

I stretched again, letting her watch my ass as I walked to the bathroom. She jumped out of the bed and wrapped the sheet around herself and trailed after me. "What do you mean together?" Her tone said she wasn't done with this conversation, which was fine with me. I was about to have some fun with this one.

"What I mean is," I said, stopping in the doorway to the bathroom. "I think we've both been fighting something we can't really put a name to." I looked at her, waiting for her to correct me. She just kept her head down, gaze on the floor. "Okay, so we agree there. I'd like the chance to see where this goes." I walked to her now and raised her chin with a single finger. "You're not just another girl, Ellie. Last night meant something. And I'd like to explore it with you. And if you don't think that's a good idea, I'll just have to convince you otherwise."

She pulled back and crossed her arms across her chest. "Isn't it the girl who's supposed to catch feelings after sex?"

I smirked at her. "We both know you felt something, too. If you had neighbors close, they would definitely know my name by now." Her face turned a deeper shade of red and she looked back down at the floor. "And," I continued. "I'm guessing you won't let me work on finding your father alone and instead of starting a war with a pack we'd probably lose to, we should just work together. And that would be a million times easier if we're not fighting." I hadn't completely thought that through, but as I spoke the words to Ellie they made even more sense to me. It would be easier to keep an eye on her if we were working together.

"Fine." She said finally, turning to walk away from me. "But no sex, just friends."

I laughed then. "We'll see what you say next time, brat. I know how to get you hot now."

She huffed rage out in a single breath as I closed the bathroom door.

Ellie

I heard the shower running and dressed quickly. I had to put distance between that gorgeous body and me. Or things would happen that would not be conducive to finding where my father was. My soul still felt raw and the realization I had already lost my brother,

I could have lost my father and I would be completely alone kept creeping up my throat until I was nearly terrified.

As I went downstairs to get coffee, I realized Bryce had come here in wolf form, which meant he had no clothes here. And the idea of him walking around my house naked again just put my nerves on edge. Because if he did, he was right. Sex would definitely happen again. Hot, wet, mind-blowing sex.

I shook that feeling off and went to the garage. Rummaging around in Tanner's old things, I found a pair of gray sweatpants the caveman upstairs could wear. As I reached the stairs going to the top level of the house, he was standing there. Still glistening from his shower, small droplets of water clinging to his pecs and abs and my mouth was suddenly dry. At least he had a towel around his waist and wasn't completely naked. "Uh . . . " I said, looking down at the sweatpants in my hand. "I found some of Tanner's things in the garage. They should fit." I walked up a few stairs, but stopped when I was eye level with that towel that hung around his hips.

"Thanks," he said as he took the pants from my hand. "Hey, while you're down there. . . " he trailed off and my eyes snapped to his. The corner of his eyes were crinkled as he was trying not to laugh.

"In your dreams, jerk-face." I turned and stomped down the stairs back to the kitchen where coffee beckoned.

I heard him laughing, but ignored him. He had stopped me from questioning Navarro's guards, he had turned my body to absolute mush that had a mind of its own and now he was walking around my childhood home like he owned the place. Rude!

"I was just going to shift back and go to the pack house," he explained as he came into the kitchen and helped himself to the pot of coffee I had on the counter. I couldn't help but notice how familiar he was with where everything was. But he had crashed here more than once in years past, having been out all hours with Tanner.

"Yeah, but now that we're working together I can drive you back and we can decide what we do next." I peaked at him over the rim of my coffee cup while I spoke, waiting for him to protest. He nodded slowly. "Okay. We can have breakfast at the pack house. It would probably be a good idea to talk to Arick."

Yeah, I knew that was coming. As part of the wolf pack, we're not to engage other packs without consent from the alpha. He wasn't going to be pleased.

"Relax," he said. "I'm only going to bring him up to speed so that you were out with me on patrol in case we picked up Harry's scent and we noticed the Navarro bunch had upped their security, too."

I frowned, curious how he had picked up on those thoughts. But then I had to remember this was Bryce. He wasn't stupid to begin with. "Why do you suppose that is, anyway?"

He shrugged and leaned against the counter. "Could be they saw we had upped our patrol, or maybe heard gossip about Harry. It is really curious, though." He gulped down the rest of his coffee. "Ready? I'm starving. Last night was quite the workout." His gaze raked over me as he spoke and I felt my chest tighten and heat pool between my legs as I remembered what exactly he had done last night. I perked up a little and smiled. "Yes, moonlight runs always take it out of me, too." He threw his head back and laughed then, seeing through me.

"Okay, brat. Let's go." He started toward me and before I thought better of it, I turned and ran to the front door, grabbing my keys on the way out. After Bryce was out and down the porch, I relocked the door and led him to the shed where I stored my car.

"Why not use the garage?" Bryce asked.

"That's for customers," I explained as I unlocked the car.

"Customers?" He looked confused. I stopped and turned toward him. The dual bay doors were behind us. "Yes," I responded and then backed away from the car. "You don't know anything about why I'm back, do you?"

He shook his head. "I guess not."

I hit the button on the fob in my hand and the bay doors began rolling up under the side of the house. I walked over and gave a grand gesture.

"Welcome to the Shadow Wolf Pack Garage." I said, proud to finally get to show it off.

"Who's the mechanic?" He asked, still not catching on.

This time I could feel I was absolutely beaming. "I am."

His jaw dropped a moment as he walked in and the lights all came on. "That's what you did instead of college?"

"Yeah. Machinery spoke to me more than matching colors, I guess. I can still use the experience for interiors of vehicles, I guess. Pick out seat material and such." I ran my hand along the engine crane and the workbench where I stood now. "I'm excited to get started."

He ran a hand through his hair and down his neck. The motion flexed his abs and I was really pissed I hadn't grabbed a t-shirt for him. "Uh, are you cold?" I asked.

He shook his head and sauntered over to where I stood against the workbench. "No, ma'am. But I am hella impressed. You're beautiful, smart and funny. The whole package." He said as his hands rested on the bench on either side of me. My breath caught in my throat as he lowered his mouth until he was just a breath away from me. "Getting you off so many times last night was like a drug, brat. And I think I'm addicted now." Before I could fully grasp his words, he was kissing me again. His tongue invaded my mouth and heaven help me, all I could do was wrap my arms around his naked shoulders and hang on as he took my senses from me and sent them soaring onto another plain of existence. He smelled of my shower gel, raw man and sexuality. He grasped my ass and lifted me as easily as he had last night until I was sitting on the bench, slightly higher than him and my knees on either side of him. This was incredibly hot and I was powerless to stop him or this. Because as much as I might protest, he was right. There was something between us, I just wasn't sure what.

While he kissed me like a hungry man, his hands easily lifted my breasts and thumbed my nipples through my bra. His hard on pressed against my belly and all I had to do was scoot just a bit closer . . .

He broke all the contact completely and stepped away, rubbing his lower lip with his thumb. "Sorry, almost forgot you said no sex."

My eyes narrowed on him. I was going to strangle him. That was how Bryce died, I was going to strangle him for being so frustrating. He looked around the garage again while I caught my breath. "This looks great. I'm sure it'll take off soon once word gets out." His eyes landed on the tarp in the far corner. I froze as my eyes followed where he was looking.

"It's Tanner's. Dad had it brought here so I could work on restoring it." My voice cracked and Bryce's eyes were on me in an instant. "I'm sorry," he offered. "I know the last day has been a lot on you." I jumped off the bench, trying to pretend I was fine. "I'll survive." I looked at the tarp again. "I know it sounds lame, but would you look at Tanner's bike with me? I haven't seen it since . . ." I trailed off, tears pooling in my eyes and I got pissed at myself.

"Sure, of course. Whenever you're ready."

I nodded and chewed my lip. But a surge of courage bubbled up my chest. "Now." I said and before I could think more of it, I walked over to the tarp and pulled a corner of the tarp. It fell away easily. I swallowed a whimper when I saw it. The front wheel was bent, the headlamp was mangled and the side mirror was shattered and hanging by a single piece of plastic. I heard Bryce stand behind me and his hands rested on my shoulders.

"I never should have said we should go for a ride that night," he said, sounding pained. He took a breath. "It's all my fault. I don't blame you for being so upset with me." His hands fell away from my shoulders.

I turned to look at him, to meet his dark gaze. It was filled with pain and regret and I suddenly realized that's what his attitude had been lately. It wasn't that he hadn't wanted me around, it was that he thought I held him responsible for Tanner's death and didn't want to have to face what he thought was there.

I looked down and turned back to the bike. "I never blamed you, Bryce. Or Arick. He was pig headed and it could have happened any night. But it was a wake up call that you three aren't immortal. Things could happen to anyone at any time. And it made life seem so fragile."

I reached out to the bike, hoping to feel some of Tanner there. I felt the grips and the brakes. The brake line fell away from the frame and dripped onto the cement under it. I reached for a shop towel and came back and dropped the towel to pick up the drips.

I examined the line closely. And I felt my breath start rushing in and out of my lungs and . . . I couldn't believe what I was seeing. "What?" Bryce asked, coming to kneel beside me.

"The line. It's a flat sever. Like it was cut." Tears of rage started falling down my face as Bryce pulled the line from my hand to look at it.

"Fuck," he said and then saw I was about to lose it. He held me close for the second time in less than 12 hours. "He didn't, he didn't, he didn't –" I was hyperventilating. "He was–"

And then everything went black.

Bryce

I drove her car to the pack house with the windows down. I was on a mission. I had called Arick from Ellie's house and brought him up to speed. "Fuck," Arick had said, letting a breath out after I explained the severed brake line. "Bring Ellie back here to the pack house, we'll figure it out."

I had looked at the couch where she was unconscious. I was glad he wanted her at the house. I couldn't stand the thought of leaving her alone after realizing her brother had been murdered. Now her father was missing and somehow, they all had to be tied together.

I disconnected from Arick and scooped her up in my arms, marveling at her for a moment. Ellie had gone away and grown into the gorgeous woman in the passenger seat beside me. But she was still Ellie. That as it turned out, she was also a mechanic, headstrong, sexy as hell and fucking amazing in bed. I felt my cock getting hard as I remembered her last night. No one had ever gotten to me the way she had. Like I didn't ever want to be away from her. And though it surprised me, last night was more than sex. She might not be my mate, but I would have her. One way or another.

I now approached the fence of the pack house and security came out to greet me, not recognizing the car.

"Mr. Bryce," The young guard said as he looked from me to Ellie, still out cold in the passenger seat.

"Do we have any of those access fobs in the shack there?" I asked through gritted teeth, not liking the way he raked his eyes over Ellie's sleeping form.

"Yes, sir." He said, snapping to attention. Scampering away from the car, he disappeared into the shack only to come back in a few moments holding the black fob in his hand. "Who should I register it to?" He asked, putting his pen to his clipboard after he handed it to me. I gave him Ellie's information and let him record the tag on her car before moving it toward the gate. Arick was right. This was Ellie. We had known her almost all her life and she wasn't some person that had just wandered into the pack. She was pack family.

I parked the car in the loop in front of the house and went to the other side of the car. I opened her door and tried to wake her by running my index finger down her face and then gently shaking her shoulder. "Ellie?"

She stirred, but didn't come to. So I scooped her up in my arms and walked up the steps to the house. The maid opened the door before I could knock, which I was grateful for. Arick met us at the bottom of the stairs. He frowned. "Still out?"

"Cold," I said as I started up the stairs, not stopping to talk to Arick.

"Where are you taking her?" Arick called out.

I hesitated a moment before answering. Honestly, I hadn't thought of it. I had just assumed I'd let her rest in my room. "She'll be comfortable in my room," I said.

Arick kind of chuckled, but let it go. "I'll meet you in your office after." Was all that he said.

I kicked my bedroom door open and made my way to the bed. Laying her down gently, I stood looking down at her longer than I thought I would. She was so beautiful laying on the dark green covers, her silver hair spilled across the dark pillows. There was something pulling at me, yearning to be next to her. Not just my wolf, but something just as deep. I knew as I turned to walk away that nothing would be the same. She was ingrained in my life, and everything would be easier if I just accepted that. Now it was going to be a challenge to get Ellie to accept it.

That she was mine now.

I knew I would have to start tracking down what had happened to Tanner's bike. Someone had cut the line, but why? And when? Obviously the night of the accident. So had someone deliberately jumped the curb? Is that why the driver was never found? Never identified? It had been dark and I couldn't see anything beyond the twin headlights. But I had ridden past it and it had taken out Tanner, who was a good two car lengths behind me. So it could have been intentional. I made a silent promise to myself and to Ellie we'd find the bastard that had done this and get answers.

Ellie

Pain began crashing against the back of my eyes as I came to. I knew I was in a bed, but not my bed. I opened one eye cautiously and looked around the darkened room and when I took a deep breath I knew where I was. This was Bryce's bed, this was Bryce's room. This was his space.

I sat straight up and instantly regretted it as pain crashed in my skull like a crescendo. I felt my face twist in a grimace, my heart racing again as I replayed last night, this morning.

Tanner's bike.

Anger quickly surged on the back of the adrenaline. Someone had messed with the bike that my brother rode, which could have changed the outcome of that accident. It suddenly started making sense that whomever hit him had never been found, why things were rushed and his funeral had been so quick. Had dad known? Is that why he was missing?

My mind was running a marathon and the pain made it difficult to pinpoint and focus on just one thought. I stumbled off the bed to the bathroom, seeking cool water from the sink to help ease the racing.

Big mistake. Bryce's laundry was in the corner, the entire room smelled like him. It flooded my senses and I felt the corners of my vision darken and I leaned against the door to try to keep my head above proverbial water. What the fuck is happening to me?

Focus, Ellie, I reminded myself and pushed myself to the large marble sink. I turned on the cold water and began splashing water on my face. I did this several times, paused and did it again. The cool water was crisp against my face and it was helping. I did this a few more times and then eyed the towel on the rack in the corner. I could dry off, but the smell of Bryce would overwhelm me again. So I opted to drip dry and left the room and made my way downstairs. Staff usually were about this time of day, but I didn't see anyone. I made my way down to the offices in the back of the house, seeking out Bryce or Arick to figure out what the big idea was bringing me here and demand to be returned to my own home. Sex didn't mean Bryce was my master or keeper now, so if he thought that's what this was, he could forget it. As I neared the doors to the facing offices of the Alpha and the Beta, I heard raised voices and paused. I knew eavesdropping was wrong, but what made me stop was I heard my name.

"I told you years ago, Arick." Grayson's voice. "That family is trouble. Harry is missing and it's causing trouble with the Navarro camp now. Do you want a war over a doctor? We can find another one. We'll bring in a human if we have to."

There was a moment of quiet and then Arick said. "Dad, I don't know what your deal is with that family, you always bitched like this when we were kids. I don't get it and frankly, I don't care anymore. Ellie has been in our lives since she was a baby and they're good people. Whatever her mother did to the pack pride is not her or Harry's fault and I won't hold them responsible."

Grayson started to speak more but Bryce now jumped in. "We will find Harry and I'll keep Ellie safe here."

I almost burst in then. I was not a child to be protected. "Over my dead body will she stay in this pack house!" Grayson shouted. "She will be fine in her own house away from Arick and Megan."

"No, she won't." Bryce said. "We found out this morning Tanner's brake line was cut and that could have led to the accident."

Grayson released a breath and there was a moment's pause. I could hear the hesitation in his voice with a hint of accusation. "And just how did you find that out? Did she tell you?"

"No, we saw the brake line and it was a clean cut. Nothing that would have happened in the accident."

"Shit," Grayson said now and I heard someone drop into a leather chair. "Why would anyone do that?"

Bryce said, "I don't know, but until I know Ellie can't be safe there. Someone was out to hurt her brother, her father is missing so presumably the same people think she'll be there alone."

"This isn't our problem, Bryce. This is a family concern. Notice only members of that family have been impacted. This isn't a pack problem." Grayson was almost whining and I clenched my fists. My heart was racing and tears burned the back of my eyes around the headache that was already pounding at my temples. I hadn't known Grayson had a problem with my family until now. But he had always set my teeth on edge.

"They are part of this pack and are loyal to this pack. Harry delivered me, for shit's sake, dad. If someone in this pack is affected, the pack is affected, and I will get to the bottom of this." Arick was firm and I recognized his alpha voice. But I didn't know if that would work on a previous alpha. It must have been because Grayson let out a breath. "Fine. But let me take Megan to the city with me until this is sorted out," he pleaded.

Everyone was quiet now. I wanted to burst in and tell them that Megan didn't have to leave her home for me, I wouldn't be staying. But before I could take a step forward Arick spoke. "Fine, but after her party. I don't want anyone to know we're onto a bigger theory. So after her party, you can take her to the city. That's not far away and we've upped the patrols. There's no reason to believe Megan is in danger right now."

I couldn't listen anymore. I needed to be out of here, finding answers.

I quickly and quietly made my way to the front of the house, still no staff in sight – thank the Moon. I opened the front door and grimaced as the bright sun hit my face and a yelp escaped me as I shielded my eyes from the sun high in the sky. My head's pounding got worse, but I was relieved my car was sitting in front of the house. I made my way down the massive steps and to the driver's side door. I was relieved that the keys were still in the ignition and I started it and had it moving before my door was closed. I was down the driveway before I looked in the mirror and saw Bryce standing at the top of the front steps, watching me. I didn't care. I needed some distance, painkillers and time to think. The gate swung open and I sped all the way home, hoping that I could make sense of the last 2 days.

I kind of laughed to myself as I settled in the driver's seat after confirming no one was following me. I hated Bryce hadn't chased me, but fuck if I knew why. I felt like a wound was opening in my chest. Like it had last night when I had crossed the point of no return and had sex with Bryce. Delicious, toe-curling sex. But it had been a mistake, it wouldn't happen again. I spent the next several minutes replaying some parts of last night, how he smelled and how he tasted and forced myself to shake it off as I drove up my gravel driveway. It was in the past. My adolescent crush finally got her wish and I slept with Bryce. Time to grow up and move on.

Chapter Eight

Bryce

I heard Arick's footsteps behind me as I watched Ellie's car disappear down the loop. He chuckled. "She really hasn't changed a bit. Still headstrong." He said, wiping up and down his face with his hand.

I felt a sense of pride puff up in my chest. Yes, she was. Headstrong, sexy, smart and incredibly beautiful. The entire package. But I didn't tell Arick that. He hadn't asked why I was carrying her unconscious from the car, or why I had been wearing only a pair of sweatpants.

I heaved a sigh and turned around, going back inside. "Yes," I said finally. "She is. But she needs to be kept safe. From everyone, including herself if I have to."

Arick was thoughtful for a minute. "She should come and stay here. Her aunt's husband is the doctor in that pack. I'll put in a call to have them come here. We can't be without a doctor, not with all the pups on the way."

I nodded as I started up the stairs. "I'll let her know to get her things together. Wish me luck."

"I don't have to wish you luck, but a metal cup to protect your balls wouldn't be a bad idea." Arick laughed as he went to the back of the house.

True. She was a spitfire and could probably bring a man to his knees. Then a smile curved my face. I needed to figure out a way to bring her to her knees.

Mate or no mate, I was going to make her acknowledge that there was something between us, even if we didn't know what that something is. As I changed my clothes, I thought through all of the arguments she was going to put up, all the reasons she'd say she couldn't stay here in the pack house. The last one I came up with made me pause. She was going to say no, she had to be there in case someone called for the doctor. The house couldn't be left empty. What if her dad called?

Realizing that, I grabbed a backpack out of my closet and threw some essentials in it. She wasn't getting rid of me that easily.

Ellie

I stood in the garage in the sun setting light. All I could do was stare at the brake line dangling from the bike. It still sent chills up my spine. Not only had someone wanted Tanner to get hurt, but they had made it happen. And it could have been the same person that had hit him head on. I knew that it was a car that had jumped the median because Bryce and Arick had seen it happen. Had watched him fly through the air where he crashed and rolled on the dark road. And the driver had just taken off, not stopping.

I heard a motorcycle approaching and it pulled me from my thoughts and as I glanced down our gravel driveway, I groaned. Why can't he just leave me alone? There was no point in going in the house and pretending I wasn't there. Not only were the bay doors open to the garage where I stood, but I hadn't put my car away for the night yet. I crossed my arms and put my forehead on my hand, wishing I had never decided to come back here, wishing my emotions hadn't gotten the better of me. Wishing I could just melt into the floor and never return. The bike came into the garage and shut off and I stared at Tanner's bike instead of acknowledging Bryce was there, in all black and larger than life. I was going to ignore the fact that my knees were weak and my heart was racing and I wondered how long I had been unconscious and if he knew I had heard what Grayson had said.

I heard Bryce take his helmet off and dismount the bike and walk toward me. Surprisingly, he put an arm around my shoulder as he too gazed at Tanner's bike. "We need to talk," he said finally.

I smiled up at him weakly. "Isn't that my line?"

He laughed for a minute. "It should be, but I wasn't the one sneaking off after waking up in my lover's bed."

I swallowed. His words made it seem so intimate. "I, uh . . . I needed to be here in case dad called."

"Did he?" He sounded sincerely hopeful.

I shook my head and turned to go back upstairs. "No. And his phone still goes to voicemail. I don't know where he is or how any of this makes any fucking sense." I could feel my blood pressure rising. This was just too much too fast. 2 days ago, I was having breakfast with an old friend and my childhood crush, then my father went missing, then I went investigating and then I was completely and totally ravished by said childhood crush and now he's in my garage. Acting like I matter.

I knew better, though. He was only interested in finding out where my father was and what this had to do with Tanner's accident. I knew somehow they were connected, but I couldn't figure it out. Doing my best to ignore Bryce, I went up the narrow stairs to the house where I made my way to my father's study. There had to be information there that explained at least some of this. But try as I might, I was painfully aware of Bryce in my house, following me down the hall and rustling around as we walked.

I went to my father's desk, careful to avoid the place by the bookcase where he had first kissed me. Deep breath, I told myself. And I sat down at the desk. One by one, I began opening drawers and sorting through papers that were there. Bryce still stood by the door, watching me with his arms folded across his chest. He hadn't removed his jacket, but the backpack was somewhere else. "I have no idea why you're here or why you're standing there. Is there something you want from me?" I heard the bitchy tone and was glad it was there. I needed to keep him at arm's length until I could sort all this out. Probably after, too. He had all but accused me of having something to do with my father's disappearance and I was sure by now he thought I had something to do with Tanner's accident, too. Which made my blood boil. Yes, they had buried their best friend, but I had buried my hero. The one person I had always looked up to, the one that had beat up the bullies at school when I had braces, the one that had held me close crying when I got my period the first time and thought I was dying. Tanner had been my everything. And now he was gone. And I didn't care what anyone else thought at this point, I was going to get answers. The pack be damned if it came down to it.

"Waiting." Was all Bryce said now.

I put the papers I was sorting down on the desk to glare at him. "I don't have time for guessing games, Bryce. Waiting for what?" The annoyance in my voice was getting more noticeable. Good, I thought. Let him know just how annoyed I am with him

"We need to talk," He said again.

"I have nothing to say. I think you've made it pretty clear that you think I had something to do with my father disappearing. Last night does not change that you thought I could turn on my own pack. Even Grayson thinks we're nothing but trouble. Just like old times." I ended on a sneer and quickly went back to shuffling through papers, though I couldn't see what was on them. My eyes were filled with tears at the pain of his low opinion of me. Why did I care? He was the beta and I was the doctor's daughter. That's it. He didn't need me, didn't want me. He just gave in to me when I pushed because I was vulnerable. So fine, he got laid. As far as I was concerned that was it.

But why did that sting like a bitch?

Because whether I wanted to admit it or not, I had still held onto my stupid girlish crush. Somewhere in the back of my mind I thought we could go on being friends and he could be a constant in my life somehow. I thought life would just pick back up where it was ten years ago. But I had been stupid and naïve. And as soon as I found my father, I was going back to the city and as far away from Bryce as I could possibly get.

He knelt beside my chair and took the papers from my hand and turned me to face him. His hands were on my knees and I just put my hands in my lap. I was angry and exhausted and my head still hurt and I was just praying he would change his mind about talking about anything and just leave.

"Ellie," he said softly and I looked into his dark eyes. It looked like genuine concern, but I didn't want to believe that. Not for a minute. "I know I acted like an ass, and I'm sorry. I don't know what Grayson's issue is. But it's his own. I don't think of you that way and neither does Arick. We are in this together." His words tore at my chest, at the walls I was working so hard to put back up and between us. I felt my eyes sting and before I could top it, a tear did slip down my face now and I swiped at it angrily.

"Ah, babygirl." He said and scooped me into his arms and carried me to the leather couch on the far wall. He tucked me under his chin on his lap as he sat down, stroking my hair. "I didn't mean to hurt you. Not once. I wish I could take it all back." He said now.

I wanted to believe him but didn't dare get my hopes up. I couldn't face disappointment now if it was just a joke he was playing on me. "You didn't. I'm just worried about Dad." I said lamely, knowing for a fact that Dad missing was only a portion of the turmoil going through me.

Bryce's chest rumbled under me as he chuckled. "We both know that's not true, Brat. This is me you're talking to. We've known each other for a really long time."

I sniffled and said nothing else as tears just flowed down my face and I strengthened my resolve to return to the city after dad came home. I felt Bryce kiss the top of my head as his hand lowered down my back and began rubbing up and down in a calming motion. Okay, I half-admitted to myself. That did feel good. "We do need to think this through, though." He said.

"Think what through?" I asked, staying cautious.

"With what we found on Tanner's bike, I don't think you're safe here. You should come stay at the pack house until we find your dad and get to the bottom of this." I stilled at his words. After a moment of hesitating – that back rub felt good – I pushed away from him to the other end of the couch.

"What the hell are you talking about?"

"Your dad is missing. And if I had a guess it wasn't a voluntary disappearance. Arick and I think the Navarro pack has something to do with it, but we can't pinpoint what. That doesn't mean he was the only one they wanted." His words made my blood run cold. It was very possible he was right, but I wasn't going to go hide with my tail between my legs until the men figured it was safe.

"I'm staying here, Bryce. I need to be here in case someone calls for the doctor. Before you ask, I have no idea how I'm going to handle it, but I will. And I need to be here in case dad makes it home."

I sat down at the desk and picked the clump of papers up again. And then the yellow slip caught my eye and I read it and frowned. "Did you find something?" Bryce asked as he got up and came to read over my shoulder.

"I thought dad had Tanner's bike all this time. But according to this receipt, he just had it brought here a few days before I got home. Where was it before that?" I asked, feeling I was looking at a piece of the puzzle, but not sure how.

Bryce shook his head when I looked at him. "I'm not sure. Arick might know, he's the one that signed for it to be hauled away from the .... accident." He said slowly, intently watching my face. "I can call him and find out, but it will cost you." He said, half smiling.

I leaned back in the chair slightly away from him. "What?"

"You have to sit down and talk to me. We need to come up with a plan. Together." His voice was stern and the playful smile was gone.

I chewed my lip for a minute. "Okay." I finally agreed. I wasn't sure exactly what the plan would be, or if it was regarding my father, my brother's bike or whatever was between him and I, but I needed answers and I would deal with that later. He stood and reached into his jacket and pulled out his cell phone and dialed Arick's. I watched him step out into the hall and took the time to read the slip again, chewing my lip. This was a receipt from a delivery service. They had picked the bike up from an address I didn't recognize and it had been brought here to this house. Dad had arranged it and signed for it when it arrived, I recognized his signature.

Could whoever cut Tanner's brake line be afraid Dad would have discovered that? A chill moved through me at the thought. What could Tanner have done or known to get into something this deep? I had more questions than answers and it was making me angry and frustrated.

Bryce approached the doorway again. "Yeah, I'll let her know. Thanks." He disconnected the call and let out a breath. "He said that his dad's cousin owns a towing and recovery service.

Grayson called them to pick it up from the scene and it's been sitting at their place for the last ten years. Arick said he can do some digging around for more information, but I told him to wait it out. If we start poking around, it could alert someone that we've found something we shouldn't have." Bryce sounded worried now. But he was right. We had to be cautious, because woman's intuition was telling me something. Is that what dad had found? I worried at my lip before I met Bryce's eyes. "Do you think this is related to dad disappearing?"

He rubbed the back of his neck. He had taken off his jacket and looked completely at home in my dad's office. But that shouldn't surprise me, he had practically grown up here. "I don't know, babe."

I tore my eyes away from him and started going through the next drawer. "Don't call me that."

I could feel his smirk at me. "Why not? Can't admit it?"

I did look at him with a "get real" eye roll. "Admit what? We did the devil's tango and it was mind blowing? Sure, it was really, really good." I started quickly flipping through papers to seem distracted, like I wasn't rattled. "Admit that there's something between us? I don't have to, because there's not. And that means no 'babe, baby' or any other pet name you may come up with. There is to be no indication that last night ever happened." I stressed that last part. I just wanted to sweep it under the rug and focus on finding my father. The sun was setting now and the office was growing dark. I reached to flip on the desk light, but Bryce's strong hand was on my wrist in the next instant, stopping me. It was a gentle grasp, but it made me look up at him. I hadn't even heard him move.

"What?" I asked, annoyed with him. Still holding my hand, he walked to behind the desk where I was sitting and pushed the drawers closed, took the papers from my hand and put them on the desk. In the next instant, he was between my knees on the floor, kneeling before me. I could feel his heat through my leggings and I regretted not wearing jeans or even something thicker. Like chainmail. Anything to add layers between us. It was then I noticed he had taken his shoes off, but I didn't comment on it. He grasped my other hand in his and drew them to his chest. "Let me get this straight," he said softly and I couldn't help but stare at his mouth as he talked. "You have a tattoo of our wolves on your back, we fucked like wild animals last night and you slept in my arms. But you expect me to believe you are okay walking away from last night without another thought?"

Holy moons I had hoped he wouldn't see the tattoo. I had just turned twenty one, drunk and sad I didn't have the trio to celebrate with. I had ended up in front of a tattoo parlor and a black wolf had stared at me through the window, the artist's pet wolf. And a yin and yang sketch had hung just behind his head. The idea had come to me then and I knew I would immortalize us the only way I would ever be able to. In a tattoo. Coming back to the present as his thumbs rubbed my hands, I tilted my chin up at him. "That's right. It was just a moment of weakness. It won't happen again."

He leaned in then and his lips were just a breath from mine. I looked down where our lips almost touched. "Ellie," he said and my gaze met his. "You're a liar." He sounded breathless as his mouth finally met mine and he began nibbling at my lips. I kept them closed, trying to resist a deeper contact, but then he dropped my hands and his hands framed my neck, his thumbs rubbing my jaw to push it open for his tongue to dance with mine. My heart was racing, I could hear our ragged breathing in the quiet of the room. It was getting darker by the second, but my care was slipping away. He held my head to his so he could kiss me, like it was all he wanted to do. His scent and taste made me dizzy and despite my better mind, I felt myself melting into his, relaxing and leaning into his touch.

His hands left my neck and wrapped around my lower back, pulling me closer to the edge of the chair, almost in his lap. This pushed my knees wider apart and I could smell my scent, the raw wetness for him. He must have smelled it as well because he moaned against my mouth and one hand reached for that part of my body. I hadn't realized how tense I was until a single fingertip pressed against me, getting my leggings and panties wet. All I could do was grasp at his massive, tan arms and pray the torment would end. In the next moment, we were like animals ripping at each other's clothes. I heard several seams rip and give way. We were desperate to touch each other's raw skin. Never breaking the kiss, he ripped my button down shirt open and buttons went flying. My bra was next, and I reached to help him with the clasp in the back, but he made little effort and the lace gave way and the next minute his mouth was on my naked breasts, his hands lifting them to his face like a feast. I could only lean back in the chair and hold onto his broad shoulders as sensations raced through me. He finally took a nipple into his mouth and I cried out as I felt my core tighten, needing desperately to be filled. "Bryce," I cried as my hands clenched in his jet black hair. I couldn't tell how long he tormented me, how long the tension in me kept building until I couldn't take it anymore. I reached for the buttons on his black jeans, but he grabbed my wrists. "Easy there, we've got time."

I whimpered as he pulled me toward his waist and stood only to kiss me again as my legs circled his waist. I held onto his shoulders and reveled in his attention, his kisses. Before I knew it, he was laying me back on my bed and I scooted away to give him room to join me only for him to go to my dresser and start looking in the top drawer.

"I –" cleared my throat. "Don't have condoms."

"Not what I'm looking for," was all he said. His back was to me so I couldn't see what he was seeking, but finally his hand landed on something and he was satisfied. He turned toward the bed, holding a belt of mine in one hand. I swallowed as I looked at it and then at him. "What's that for?" I asked, my voice cracking.

"To prove a point," was all he said and he climbed on the bed with me. He put the belt aside and started kissing me again, but my mind was racing with what he was about to do. He kissed down the side of my neck, stopping to bite me and I was sure that was going to leave a mark but it felt so delicious, I didn't care. I just wanted this ache to continue and stop at the same time. My skin felt like it was on fire. He took his pants off and was gloriously naked now, having shed his shirt downstairs.

He climbed between my legs and removed my leggings and panties. It was then he kissed my belly ring and lifted my ass up until he was drinking from me again, just like last night. I cried out and arched my back off the bed, wanting the contact to deepen. But he hovered and just lightly blew on me, sending chills all over me. I grabbed for anything I could find until finally latching onto his hair and arching toward his face. The next moment, he had both of my wrists in his hand and surged up my body to hold my hands above my head. The other hand grabbed my chin and turned me to face him. I felt his erection between my legs and I wiggled, trying to take him in. I was so focused on him not being in me that I didn't feel him secure my hands to the headboard with the belt he'd taken from the drawer. I fought against the restraint, but it was secure. I looked at him then. "This is the lesson?" I panted at him as excitement danced through me. My breathing became extremely labored and heat spread through me.

"Part of it. Be patient, brat." He then began trailing kisses down my throat until he was sucking hard at my nipples, which made me moan and writhe, tugging at the belt on my wrists. I knew I was beyond wet and this ache was almost unbearable.

"Bryce . . ." I pleaded.

"You're not ready yet." He said, lifting his head from my chest to look at me. "Would you like a taste of what you're in for?" He asked, smirking at me. But this smirk was different. It was from a man who knew how to control my body, how to get out of it what he wanted, what he craved. "Answer me." His voice was quiet but firm.

I nodded, holding my breath. I felt his hand brush between my legs and then he turned his wrist and just his thumb entered me. It wasn't deep contact, it was meant to drive me crazy. And it was succeeding. He moved it so slightly and I was ready to start crying. The sensations were delicious but not what I needed, what I craved.

I arched against his hand, trying desperately to deepen the contact. He kept the contact shallow as he sucked at my nipple, driving me even closer to the brink without pushing me over. I have no idea how long he did this to me as I fought against my restraints, as I tried to deepen the contact. Finally he stopped and pulled away before lowering his face to between my legs. "Are you ready to admit it?" He said and I felt his breath dance across my already sensitive skin.

I swallowed, coming to my senses. "Admit what?" I was so confused and I felt drunk.

"Admit there is something here. Something deeper than we would have thought was possible ten years ago."

I shook my head. "It's just sex," I lied. It was so much more than that. He had all of my trust, he knew how to command my body and I was powerless against it. But I wouldn't tell him that.

"Have it your way," He said with a grin as he dragged his tongue across my clit. I cried out and arched against his mouth. He did this at least a hundred more times, each time taking me closer to the edge. "Bryce, please. . ."

"Please what?" He looked at me, I could feel his gaze.

"Please, I want you so bad."

"So you admit it?" His finger grazed over my clit again and I cried out. "Yes! I admit it."

"Ah, good girl. Say you're mine." He moved up my body and was nibbling at my neck, stroking my nipple with one of his hands.

"Oh God, Bryce . . ." I kept arching against him.

"Say it, Ellie. Say you're mine."

I had no idea what this would gain him, but even as I resisted saying the words I knew he was right. There would be no one else in my life after him. "I'm yours." I finally agreed.

He braced his body against mine and raised up on his elbows to face me, positioned to enter me. "Look at me, Ellie. I want to watch you come on my cock."

I did as he told me to and in the next moment he entered me. I cried out at the sensation of being filled and I felt my body clench around his repeatedly. He moved slowly at first, his gaze locked with mine as he claimed me as his in a ritual that was as old as time. He only moved in me a handful of times before my world was spiraling and I cried out as I came around him. He stopped moving then, just holding me as my orgasm shuddered through me. He was still in me and I was trembling at the power of my release, but I was still unable to hold him. My hands were still in the belt above my head.

He kissed the underside of my breast and held me still, feeling me spasm around him. Then he took my nipple in his mouth and bit gently and I cried out and arched into it. "Mmmm. Good girl." His hips ground against me and I felt tension beginning to mount low in my belly at the sensations. He was right, I realized then. My body belonged to him and he could do anything to me he wanted. All I knew was I wanted him to keep doing this to me as long as he could. Then he was moving faster and faster. I felt myself climbing again and I pushed against his pelvis, trying to take all of him that I could. When I was almost there, he sat back and lifted my legs in the air, resting one ankle against his shoulder as he pumped into me extremely fast, pounding against my body. All I could do was watch his strong muscles in the dwindling light as he held me in place to take his pleasure from me. I felt the tension quickly mount and I cried his name again as I came and he stiffened between my legs, crying out my name before collapsing on me, his own release deep in my body now.

He collapsed on top of me, pressing me into the mattress like a heavy weighted blanket. Both of our breathing was ragged, we were both spent and I was getting tired. But at the same time, I wanted to go hide and cry. This changed everything, and I was feeling extremely vulnerable. The passion between us was strong. So much stronger than I had ever dreamed of as a stupid adolescent girl. And no matter what happened now, he was a piece of me. He claimed to want me as well. But we weren't mated, so what would happen if our mates came along? One of us or both would be broken-hearted.

Bryce pushed up on his elbows and kissed me then. He broke the kiss and reached up and released my wrists from the belt and I rubbed my wrists absently to keep from wrapping my arms around him and holding him. "Did it hurt you bad?" He asked, his brow creased with a worried expression on his face.

I smiled at him, aching everywhere. "Not terribly. It was a good hurt."

He slid off me to my side and pulled me close to him and kissed me, his big hand rubbing my hip over to my ass where he grabbed a handful. "So beautiful," he sighed as he flopped on his back, bringing me with him. I was tense beside him as he stroked my back with his arm.

He looked at me. "I meant what I said, Ellie."

"What?" I was hoping he meant something else. Anything else.

"You're mine now. I should have found you before now and I didn't. And I'm sorry."

I didn't say anything and he rolled back on his side to face me. "Why are you trying to resist this?"

I worried my lip and searched in the darkness for the words. "We're not mated. What happens if your mate stumbles into your path tomorrow?"

He cupped my face in his hand and kissed me tenderly. "I'll reject her. I only want you."

His words did things to me that I didn't want to think about or admit. "I don't know that I can handle you not rejecting her. I've lost my brother, I might have lost my dad. I've lost more in this life than anyone ever should. You've always treated me like a sister and been a missing piece in my life. I don't want this to get complicated." I felt like I was word vomiting, but I felt vulnerable and here in the dark with Bryce I felt safe to share my thoughts and my feelings.

"I get it. But what you're making me feel is so amazing, I'm willing to take that chance." He released a breath. "Don't forget, I have the same risk in this you do. You could find your mate tomorrow and I don't think he'd be thrilled with the idea of you hanging around me." His words rang in my ears. I hadn't thought of that. I had been so wrapped up in Bryce that my mate had never crossed my mind. I knew that I would reject him if he came into my path. As a girl, this had been all I'd ever wanted, for Bryce to return my feelings.

"I'm not going to lose you now, Ellie. I've been alone my entire life and these feelings are still new but I want to give them a chance. I hope you'll let me show you that you won't regret this. Let me earn your affection." I felt my jaw drop. Big bad Bryce spilling his guts over little old me? This was surreal. I must be dreaming.

I let out a light laugh and I felt his smile in the dark. "What's funny?"

"I've been half in love with you my entire life. Do you know how many times I laid in this very bed and dreamt of the mighty Bryce spilling his guts and pleading for a chance with me?"

"Well," he said, flopping back on the pillow. "I spilled my guts because you let me rearrange yours."

"Bryce!" I yelled, punching at his shoulder. This kind of banter was so new and fun and freeing, like a weight had been lifted off my chest and I could start breathing again. He laughed and pulled me close. The kiss deepened and got more urgent and I climbed on top of him, straddling his waist. He was already hard and I was eager to take him in me again and it was so simple to ease on top of him and take him deep. I grasped the headboard and his hands cupped my breasts as I rode him, feeling free and so full of new emotion I couldn't think beyond this moment with him.

And as we came together, crying out in the darkness I knew there was no going back. We were tied together, whether I liked it or not.

Chapter Nine

Bryce

I watched her sleep, the half-moon light spilling in her curtains to give a faint illumination to the room. I wasn't sure what my next steps were as far as she was concerned. Because she was right, our mates were out there somewhere still. I knew I wouldn't want anyone other than Ellie, she was a home I hadn't realized I'd had until she left and came back into my life.

As kids, she had been my constant. The one thing I could count on. Whether she was tagging along with her brother or spying on us from upstairs as we laid as wolves in Tanner's back yard, she was always around, always there. And not having a family of my own outside of Arick, I hadn't realized the void she had filled in my life. She had become a part of who I was, and the part of me that had been missing the last 10 years I hadn't recognized.

I heard a wolf's howl from the hill behind the house then, drawing my attention from her sleeping form. I carefully got out of bed and went to the window, not bothering with clothes as I moved the curtains aside and looked out over the hill. It was Damon on patrol. He was undoubtedly checking on me. Once I signaled I was fine, he turned and ran into the woods to continue his patrol. I knew Damon would tell the others I was here with Ellie and word would start circulating around town, but I didn't care. Let them talk. As long as they knew she was mine. I went back to the bed, standing over her.

The Cielo pack had agreed to send their doctor to us and Ellie's aunt Tessa was undoubtedly coming along to keep up with Ellie, from what Arick had said. Thank the moon for marriage bonds to other packs. Without Tessa's bond with that pack, the pups coming into the world could be in danger.

It wasn't uncommon for mothers and pups to die in birthing, and medical assistance was usually required. Before I realized what I was thinking, I started picturing Ellie big with my child in her. Would she welcome that? It was hard to say. She was here to be the pack mechanic, and that would be hard growing with a child and then caring for an infant.

I shook it off. If we were not mates, no children would come from us being together. Part of me was fine with that, part of me was disappointed at the thought. As I stood mulling over our future together, which I would see to making it happen, the hair on my arm stood on end. I held my breath, listening and then I heard a soft click come from downstairs.

My heart started to pound in my ears and I pulled on my jeans. I shook Ellie's shoulder. "Ellie?" I whispered in her ear. She stirred and opened her mouth to say something. I placed a hand over her mouth which startled her. "Shh. There's someone downstairs. Stay here." She nodded her understanding, her eyes wide open and her breathing rushed.

I quietly moved to the door, picking up her metal bat leaning against the frame and opened the door and crept to the top of the stairs. I saw a shadow move from the front door to the office where Ellie and I had been just hours before. It was human and dressed in several layers, so I wasn't able to pick up a scent of any kind. With the bat in hand, I made my way down the stairs prepared to square off against the intruder. But the floorboard creaked three steps from the bottom and I grimaced, wondering if the intruder heard it. I don't know how long I stood there waiting, but then I heard papers rustling in the office and I knew I hadn't been discovered. I eased my back against the hallway wall as I made my way down to the office, careful with how fast I put my weight on each board to avoid a noise. As I was getting to the office, the shadow nonchalantly opened the office door and began making their way down the hallway. I swung the bat in complete darkness, hoping to connect with something that would slow them down.

It did connect, but not where I wanted obviously. The shadow recovered quickly and grabbed the bat, lifting it above my head and then a hard fist landed square in my sternum, sending me flying back against the wall. I twisted and pulled the bat over my head and the assailant was on his back and I landed a punch in his face before he wiggled away and ran down the hallway. He flung open the door and ran out where a motorcycle was waiting and cut it on. I ran as fast as I could to get outside, but a white blur ran down the stairs and past me.

"Stop!" I heard Ellie scream and my blood ran cold. Had she gotten hurt in the mix and I hadn't realized it? The motorcycle started and revved before taking off, spewing gravel everywhere. I saw Ellie turn her head to avoid it in her eyes and then raised her gun and squeezed off a single shot. There was a second loud pop almost instantly and the back tire blew out and threw the rider over the handle bar and into the gravel, skidding off into the darkness. Before he had stopped moving, Ellie was running down the driveway, wearing just my t-shirt with her gun aimed on the shadow trying to crawl into the darkness. "Don't move, fucker!" She yelled, her voice loud and extremely firm. I was amazed, proud and extremely turned on by her show of power. The shadow kept moving, grunting and she fired another shot and the shadow was still.

Scared someone might be waiting in the bush, I ran to her side. I found she had shot near his head and he was now frozen in fear with his hands up. I grabbed the back of his neck and picked him up, twisting an arm behind his back to make sure he didn't go anywhere. I ripped off his ski mask. I didn't recognize him in the half moon light, but I was going to get answers. Ellie kept the gun in her hand and followed us to where the motorcycle laid on its side. It was more of a small dirt bike. Disposable. I looked at it in the dim porch light. Even with gravel flying at her face, she had shot the back tire and thrown the rider. Pride made my chest swell, and I would make sure she knew later just how impressed I was at her skill.

The shadow I was holding started wiggling and I tightened my grip on his arm, letting him know I was willing to break his shoulder. He still hadn't gathered his breath from being thrown and I smelled blood, so something was bleeding. Ellie went into the house ahead of us, turning on lights as she went.

"Take him to the garage. We can secure him to the engine crane." The chill in her voice was not the Ellie I had grown up with, not the one that had answered the door earlier this week looking like country sunshine, not the woman I had just made scream and orgasm until she couldn't breathe. This was another Ellie I hadn't met yet.

I paused only a minute as she opened the garage door and made her way down the stairs, still safely holding what I see now was a Glock. She went to the far side of the shop and got a roll of tape and a pack of zip ties. After setting the supplies near the engine crane, she aimed the Glock at our shadow friend and cocked an eyebrow. "Whatever is running through that shit you call a brain, don't try it." She leaned just a little closer as she said, "we both know I know how to use this."

Our friend was silent as I secured him on the floor. In the light of the garage, I saw that his nose was bleeding and several layers of his clothes were ripped and torn. I ripped the right sleeve of his black sweater to reveal his pack tattoo.

"Shit," Ellie breathed.

It wasn't a tattoo I recognized. A wolf howling at the moon with a crimson crescent moon behind it. At my confused look she shook her head. "He's hired a gun out of Cielo pack." She explained to me before glaring at the man in front of us. His face was dark, his eyes circled with dark grease to help him hide in the dark. His black hair was shaggy from the ski cap he'd been wearing. "Who hired you?" She asked him.

He spat to her. "I ain't telling you shit, punta."

Before I could react, she reared back with the gun and swiped it hard across his face. I couldn't hide my shock fast enough and I'm sure our guy saw it. He spit blood out and I'm pretty sure I heard a tooth rattle. "That's not a nice way to talk to a lady. Didn't your bitch of a mother teach you any manners?" Ellie said now, not the least phased by the insult. She then turned to me, nodding approval for me to step in. Which I didn't need, but this obviously wasn't her first time dealing with this type. "You might wanna speak up there, pal. She looks really pissed."

To punctuate her point, I heard the gun click another one into the chamber. It was hard to say what she was thinking, but it was very clear Ellie wasn't playing.

"I ain't got anything to say to you, amigo. My lips are sealed."

I released a breath and then walked to the front of the garage and opened the doors. Ellie didn't say anything as she watched me step out into the early morning light and howl. As I walked back into the garage, I heard several howls go up and knew several were coming. I was thankful when Arick and Damon's wolves came into the garage, flanked by two other wolves. Ellie nodded at them and I saw Arick take her in and linger on the gun in her hands. His eyes met mine and I nodded with a firm expression.

Ellie clicked the safety in place and set the Glock on the counter, obviously feeling secure. She walked over to Tanner's boxes of things in the corner. She found a box of his clothes and set them on the ground. "These are a little tight on Bryce," she addressed the pack. "But maybe you can find something that'll do."

She then took the gun and went upstairs, leaving me with a bunch of unanswered questions.

But also a larger sense of pride in my woman. My woman.

Chapter Ten

Ellie

Arick had told me to rest in his wolf form, and I had to follow orders because he was Alpha. But I didn't have to like it. I laid down on my bed and replayed it all in my mind. I didn't recognize the intruder, but there is a good chance he knew who I was. Most of the Cielo pack knew about me from my time with Matt. It was only a matter of time before I had to tell a really long story to Bryce, and I wasn't ready to face that part of me. The part of me I had left in the city for the last ten years of my life.

The sun was creeping over the horizon and the sky was turning shades of pink and purple as it welcomed the dawning day. I laid in bed looking at it from where I was propped against my pillows. I had made the bed and laid on top of the covers. There was a burning in the pit of my stomach to get answers, to beat this bastard to within an inch of his life until he gave answers. Who hired him? Did he know where my father was? What was he looking for in the study?

The last question had me sitting up and in motion. I quickly dressed in jeans and put a bra on, which my breasts were grateful for.

I pulled on a sage green t-shirt and padded downstairs in my bare feet. I heard raised male voices coming from the garage and there were several loud thumps, which means the pack was taking care of business. I turned away from the sounds and went to my father's office. It wasn't destroyed like I had thought it would be, but the desk had been rifled through. I quickly flipped through the papers I found, hoping I'd be able to pinpoint what was missing.

"Ellie?" Bryce called from the top of the stairs. I let the sound of his voice saying my name bring me some calm and closed my eyes for a moment. "In here," I called back.

The next instant, Bryce was pulling me into his arms. He held me tight and smoothed my hair. I relaxed into his embrace and let him hold me. I wasn't sure what had brought on this comfort, but I also hadn't realized how much I wanted to be reassured everything was okay. He pulled away from me before kissing me very tenderly. Like we hadn't seen each other in years. "Are you okay?" I asked, looking him over. He now had a black t-shirt that I didn't remember from yesterday and his jeans still hung low on his hips.

He cupped my neck and I pulled his hands away to hold them. Then I saw the rough shape his knuckles were in. They were bloody and battered. "What happened? Did he say anything?" I asked, my eyes searching his for hope.

"He didn't give up anything. You're sure he's Cielo?" He pinned me with a look that told me he needed to be absolutely sure. I nodded. "Yes, that's the seal of that pack. But the red moon means he crossed the alpha and wasn't part of the pack anymore. He could be from anywhere, they usually follow the money." I stepped away before he saw too much in my eyes. I wasn't ready for this, for any of it. But then again, I wasn't sure I'd ever be ready for my father to go missing, my house to be broken into and a beta wolf taking up most of my thoughts and personal space.

Bryce cleared his throat. "Arick wants to see Tanner's bike if that's okay with you."

I took a deep breath and nodded but didn't say anything, I just went to the garage. When I ascended the stairs, all of the wolves looked at me. There was something in their eyes that made me uncomfortable, but I didn't let it get to me. The bay doors were open and the morning sun was high in the sky, spilling light into the area. I did notice our new friend wasn't anywhere in sight and that made me nervous.

"He's gone," Arick offered as I eyed the crane where he had been tied up. I nodded and moved to Tanner's bike in the corner. Bryce must have put the tarp on it while I was upstairs and I was grateful for that because I hadn't had the energy to face it again. My eyes stung now as I reached for the tarp and I prayed I wouldn't actually cry as I removed it.

Arick moved to the bike and lifted the line and ran his thumb over the clean cut. He clenched his fist around the cord and muttered something I couldn't understand, but I didn't ask him to repeat it. One, because he was grieving his best friend and two because I didn't want to risk my voice cracking. I hadn't let myself deal with the fact that it wasn't just fate that had taken my brother from me. Someone had been behind it and purposefully took him from me, from our family.

As we all stood in silence, our heads bowed in silent mourning I heard a car approaching. I looked out the bay doors toward the front of the house and shielded my eyes from the sun. I didn't immediately recognize the vehicles and I felt Bryce come stand behind me, his hands on my shoulders. And then I recognized the three black SUVs approaching. I prayed the ground would just open up and swallow me whole.

"Do you know them?" Bryce asked, his grip tightening on my shoulders as I looked heavenward for a way out. Maybe I could have a heart attack and be spared the next few moments I was sure that would span an eternity.

"Yes," I answered after carefully choosing my words. "It's my aunt, her son and the Alpha of Cielo."

Arick was coming to stand with us as the vehicles came to a halt in front of the bay doors where we were. The 1st vehicle's rear passenger door opened and out stepped the Alpha. He stood a towering 6 feet tall, raw muscle hidden under his suit, black hair slicked back as it brushed the collar of his white shirt. The bowstring tie he'd chosen tied in perfectly with the thick woven black rope around each wrist like bands of authority. His dark skin was drinking up the sun, his eyes scanning the area as he walked to the garage where we stood. He nodded at me and finally smiled/smirked. "Hey, Ellie." He said casually and I felt Bryce stiffen behind me. There was no mistaking his familiarity with me.

"Hello, Matt. Long time no see." I kept my tone formal and cold.

"That is solely your doing," he said, taking a step closer to me. "You know you have a standing invite anytime." I cleared my throat and stepped back, Bryce moving between us.

"Alpha," Arick said, ducking into the conversation smoothly. "I appreciate you sending us help on such short notice." He extended his hand, but Matt's gaze lingered on me a moment before he shook Arick's hand. "Any pack of Ellie's is a pack of mine." He said with a charming smile and I rolled my eyes.

I wasn't proud of the fact my ex-boyfriend was the alpha of my aunt's pack. I had ended whatever relationship we'd had when he took the role after his father died suddenly of a heart attack. Matt hadn't wanted to be alpha and had shrugged it off until he couldn't any longer. The pack needed a leader; Matt's uncles and cousins had all started circling the throne of power after Terrence had passed away and Matt had been concerned that in their quest for power the pack would suffer. They already had grandeur of power over other packs and Matt had no interest in expanding the territory of the Cielo pack. "Oh, you know Ellie well?" Arick asked, trying to keep the conversation light. I could feel Matt's gaze rake over me and I avoided meeting his eyes, choosing to look at my folded hands. I could hear the smirk in his voice. "Ellie and I go way back. Don't we?" I chanced a glance at Bryce. His jaw was clenched, and his fists were tight. Arick was looking from Bryce to me to Matt. He was trying to figure out next steps without pissing anyone else off, but he looked uncomfortable. And that wasn't a good look on Arick.

I cleared my throat. "Matt and I dated for a while when I lived in the city."

Matt clicked his tongue. "I think we did more than that. She would have been Luna if she had just said yes."

"But," Bryce said, glancing at me. "She said no. Lady made her choice."

"That she did. And stuck to it." Matt sighed and removed his sunglasses and made a sweeping motion. "But I'm so glad that she put the knowledge I gave her to good use. This shop looks like it's going to really make you work up a sweat. We always had fun doing that, remember?"

I just wanted a big gaping hole to open right under my feet. I was ready to go, I'd had a good life. I rubbed my forehead where a headache was starting. "It's very kind of you to pay us a visit. Are you here on business?" I hoped he would just go with that flow of conversation.

Matt took a deep breath before looking Bryce up and down. "Well, Alpha Arick called and asked for help. And I'm not one to send my pack out without me seeing what's going on, first. And then I heard that this morning someone with our pack ink on him tried to break in here. But then Ellie set him right." He winked at me and there was no mistaking the pride in his eyes as he looked me from head to two. He then glanced around the garage. "Where is he, anyway?"

Arick squared his shoulders, ready for whatever would come next. "We handled it."

Matt clicked his tongue again. "I must insist that I do my best to handle it. Kade." I hadn't noticed his beta, Kade walked into the garage. His skin was fairer than Matt, but his beard was just as dark. His head was shaved smooth today, but I had seen it buzzed extremely close in the past and knew his hair was as dark as his beard. He wore a black tank top, black jeans and really big black boots. His arms were covered in full sleeve tattoos and his gray eyes said he had seen things. I had never had the nerve to ask what he had seen for fear of nightmares. Pretty sure Kade was the thing of many wolves' nightmares.

Arick looked around at his wolves, all half dressed in ill-fitting clothes. He nodded with his chin. "He had a rough morning. We were letting him sleep it off around the corner. You know, out of sight." Kade nodded and went around the corner. The air was tense as we waited to hear his reaction. My head was full on pulsating now. I heard some scuffling around the corner and then a man screamed. I moved to see what was going on, but Bryce was still in front of me and wouldn't let me. As Kade brought him around the corner, I saw the intruder's face was swollen and bloody. "Do we know him, Kade?" Matt asked, looking at the man Kade was holding by his shirt. "No, but they messed his face up pretty good. Did he give up anything, Alpha Arick?" Kade's tone was incredibly respectful, and I felt a small spark of pride. My experience with Kade had always made me think of a caveman, so I was impressed he could be respectful and polite to my alpha.

"He didn't give us anything. We still don't know why he was here or what he was looking for." Arick answered. Matt turned to Arick, half smirking. "Kade will get information out of him." With a single flick of his wrist, Matt waved him off. Kade shuffled the intruder into the back of the last SUV and climbed behind the wheel and left. "How did you catch him, Alpha?" Matt asked, folding his glasses and putting them inside his jacket pocket.

Arick nodded at Bryce. He took a step more to my right, trying to block me completely from Matt. "Ellie shot his back tire out as he was trying to get away." He sounded extremely proud, but I couldn't see his expression. I heard Matt laugh and looking over

Bryce's shoulder I saw Matt's head thrown back. "That's Ellie for you. She was always a good shot." He turned to me peeking over Bryce's shoulder and saluted me with two fingers. "Hat's off, El. Amazing as always." He blew me a kiss and Bryce stiffened. Matt then looked at Bryce. "I don't think we've met, wolf." Matt said, almost sneering.

"This is my beta, Bryce." Arick said for Bryce.

Now it was Bryce that reminded me of a caveman as he grunted. "Well, well, well." Matt said as I shoved past Bryce and glared at him. "So you didn't want to be a luna, but a beta's bitch is fine?"

My breathing was rushing in at his words and before I knew it, my hand connected with his face. "You might be an alpha, Matt. But you do not come into my home and disrespect me."

Matt rubbed his face. "That's fair, my apologies." I heard the breath Arick had been holding whoosh out of his chest. Matt looked at Arick, then Bryce, then me. "We had some good times, El. I don't want there to be bad blood between us." He stroked my cheek then. "You know, just in case you decide to change your mind about my offer." I grasped his hand in mine and firmly returned it to his space. "That won't happen. And you know why."

"Well, no need to rehash this. I have some business to discuss with Alpha Arick." He turned to Arick then. "I would be happy to give you a ride back to your pack house so we can discuss formalities, if that is fine with you."

Arick raised his chin. "That's very kind of you, Alpha. I would be appreciative. My wolves are tired." He looked at Bryce.

"Beta, make sure the doctor gets settled here and has everything they need."

Bryce nodded. "Yes, Alpha."

It was weird watching them being so formal to each other, but I could only guess as to the reason why. And I really didn't care. I just wanted all this testosterone out of my house.

"Thank you, Matt. The pups will be safe under the doctor's supervision." I said as I moved past him. He did a mocking bow and left my garage, taking all of my pack with him except Bryce.

I sank onto the stairs as Bryce closed the garage bay doors and came toward me.

"It's my cousin that's come. He knows the house. I just need a minute." I moved to one side so he could go upstairs, but instead he sat down next to me.

He raked a hand through his hair and braced his elbows on his knees. "You didn't tell me your ex was the alpha."

I wanted to just groan, curl up and die. "It didn't matter. I broke it off when he took alpha. He's not my mate and I knew his mate would come along eventually if he wasn't so damn pig headed to avoid it. And I didn't want to be Luna." That was the truth through and through. Being a Luna was planning and handling an entire pack of worries. I loved being a mechanic and fixing things, in the thick of the day-to-day. I was not Luna material.

He nodded but didn't say anything. "He seemed to know a lot about you."

I rubbed my temples clockwise as I considered my words carefully. "Yes, we dated for about 4 years. I moved out of my aunt's house to be with him. He didn't want to be alpha and we had a lot of fun. He taught me a lot of what I know about engines and helped me get the knowledge I needed for the rest. He arranged my work for me and kept me safe." I had acknowledged then that Matt and I weren't mates, but something about him rejecting the role of Alpha to be a lone wolf had been attractive and his risky bad boy mentality had been refreshingly new and yet similar to Bryce.

"Safe enough you had to learn how to use guns?" He asked, his concern was apparent. The expression on his face belied the conflict he was feeling. On one hand, I suppose I understood. It was another man teaching what Bryce was now calling his woman things. On the other hand, I had my own brain and could manage on my own fine without a man. I took a deep breath before explaining further. "No, safe enough that I didn't. But I didn't want to rely on just him. I needed to prove I could stand on my own and didn't need anyone hovering all the time." The idea of being a scared female the rest of my life, like I had been when I ran away from this house. That fear had driven me to Matt and then I forced myself to learn to take care of myself.

Bryce nodded. "There's still a lot of things I have questions on, but that's a good start." He put his arm around my shoulders and pulled me close. "I'm sorry I wasn't there the last ten years."

I pushed away from him. "You don't have to apologize. I had to grow up some time." It came across colder than I had intended, but I wanted to make sure he knew that anything between us was new and he wasn't my protector. I looked at the bay doors and back to him. "You should be with Arick. As the beta. I don't want the dynamic of the pack impacted because of me."

Bryce frowned and looked at the bay doors and then to me. "I'm not going anywhere knowing someone just tried to break in here again while you were asleep."

I offered him a weak smile, not willing to admit I was a little rattled, too. "I'll be fine. But if you're not there to find out what Kade gets out of our break-in artist then I have to be. Because I want to know where my father is and that asshat might know." I stood now, letting him know I mean business. Matt now had the only lead on where dad was and I wasn't about to let that go.

Bryce searched my eyes and knew I was serious. He stood from the steps and cupped my chin. "I'll be back once I have information. You have the fob to the pack house gate in your car. Use it if you don't feel safe or just text me." He kissed me then and it felt a lot like a goodbye kiss. Like I wouldn't see him again. Somehow, I wasn't surprised. Their lives had been fine until I came back here. Even Dad's life was in danger because of me.

"It's not goodbye, I'm just really going to miss you." He whispered as he rested his forehead on mine and I felt a warmth bloom in my stomach. This tender side of Bryce was new to me. But I was really starting to like it. He hugged me one more time, taking a deep breath against my skin before going up stairs. I went to go cover Tanner's bike.

As the tarp fell into place, my aunt came down the stairs with her son in tow. "Ellie!" She cried as she pulled me into an embrace. It felt good to see her again, it had been awhile since I'd moved out of her house to live with Matt. Over my aunt's shoulder, I waved at my cousin, Wade. He was well over 6 foot tall, in shape and a full sleeve of tattoos came down his left forearm to where his watch glinted in the light. His black hair was slicked back into a ponytail today and his white Def Leppard t-shirt was tucked into dark blue jeans, which lay over white sneakers. I had always been impressed with my cousin. He looked tough enough to medically treat a wolf but had a great bed-side manner that calmed people down. I was surprised Matt had chosen Wade to be our pack doctor until my father came back, but I wasn't going to look a gift horse in the mouth. My aunt pulled away from the hug and grasped me by the shoulders. She was just a bit shorter than me, her silver hair was peppered with white already but her sharp blue eyes showed that with her age came wisdom. My mother's sister was kind, caring and warm. Being raised by a man and my brother, I hadn't really known what to do with that affection and I know I drove her crazy at least once.

"It's good to see you, Aunt Tessa." I said now. And I really meant it. Being in the house that screamed at me that Tanner and Dad were gone was more torture than I was ready to bear. "I'm surprised that Matt sent you, Wade. Thank you for coming."

Wade crossed his arms over his chest and looked down. "I don't mind coming, but Matt wanted me here to keep an eye on you."

I closed my eyes and counted to ten quietly. I was too tired to really act on it, but this was annoying information, even if it wasn't surprising. Matt had tried more than once to get me to be Luna of the Cielo pack, even though we were not mated. I couldn't be what a Luna needed to be. I wasn't a hostess, I wasn't lady like. I wasn't a diplomat's wife, for sure. And Matt deserved someone that would make him proud and if I'm being completely honest, it didn't break my heart to end our relationship. Part of me had never let go of Bryce fantasies and it wasn't fair to Matt to keep him at arm's lengths when there was a deeper connection out there. "Relax," Wade said now. "From the notes and files upstairs, I'm going to be busy with all the pups due in the coming months. What I don't see or hear, I don't see or hear." He finished that with a wink and turned toward the stairs. "Now come on, I'll cook dinner and we'll catch up."

Chapter Eleven

Bryce

I sat to the right of my Alpha, side eyeing our guest at the other end of the table. His crew lined the long dining table as staff fussed and carried on with the meal. I felt my jaw clenching repeatedly and I had to force myself to try to relax . In other times, I could see how people liked Matt. He was charming, jovial and relaxed as he drank the pack wine and joked with Arick. But I knew he had a past with Ellie and that burned my ass worse than anything. He had hinted several times in Ellie's garage that she had a standing invitation to go back to the Cielo pack and be his Luna. My fist clenched again as I thought of her walking away from all this with our pack to be with Matt.

I felt my fist slam into the table as Matt laughed at something Arick had just said. Everyone at the table looked at me and I was trying to give a shit and not rush to Matt and begin pummeling his face until he wasn't a pretty boy anymore.

Arick shot me a look. "You'll have to excuse Bryce, Alpha. He's not had much sleep due to overseeing the patrols."

Matt cleared his throat and sat his wine glass down. "Understandable." He wiped his lips with the napkin before returning it to his lap. What a gentleman, I scoffed inwardly. "If I may be so bold, I do have a few questions for your beta." I looked at him as he leaned back in his chair, completely relaxed as he eyed me. I met his gaze, not at all afraid. I could definitely take this city wolf.

Arick was stiff in his chair as he made a sweeping motion. "Of course, we are happy to answer anything you want to know."

"Your patrols take you to Ellie often, Bryce?"

Don't even think about it. Arick's voice echoed in my head as my vision darkened and all I saw was the pulse in his neck from this distance. I dreamed of ripping his throat out and howling with satisfaction as he breathed his last. Just the sound of her name from him made me see red.

"Yes, since her father disappeared. I've been keeping an eye on her." My voice was low, quiet and it dared him to ask more questions.

We can only trust him so far, he may be trying to use Ellie to distract you. Remember, it was his pack that broke into her house last night. Arick's voice was deep in my head and the only thing keeping me in this reality.

Matt nodded now. "Alpha Arick, I must insist I have some wolves join your beta on patrols. It will help them learn the territory and the boundaries. With them being so new to the area, I don't want a mistake that could start a war." Matt smiled and I knew this was to be nothing but a cock block. To keep tabs on my interactions with Ellie at night.

Arick nodded. "That makes sense." He cut a sharp glance to me as I looked away from Matt before I did something that *would* start a war. "I had asked Ellie to come stay with us until we knew she was safe, but she's extremely stubborn." *I'm going to send Damon to keep guard at the house so Matt and his wolves stay away.* Arick reassured me.

Matt laughed again, throwing his head back. "Yes, she is. I've had to discipline her more than once in the short time she was mine."

His words threw me into a rage and I stood, the chair flying behind me quickly before thudding into the wall of the dining hall. A hush fell over the dining hall and everyone was holding their breath. Matt raised an eyebrow as I stood bowed, ready to kill him. "Alpha Arick, I believe I've angered your beta. My deepest apologies," he said this mockingly, picking his wine glass up again.

"It's just been a long day, Alpha." Arick offered. *Rest tonight, you've had a long day. Leave us.* He ordered me.

Arick was pissed at me, but I didn't care. Matt wasn't going to leave here alive if I had my way. Now, Arick commanded in my head and I couldn't disobey. As I went upstairs, I heard them laughing and shook my head. It would be a shame if anything happened to him while he was here, I sneered at the thought.

At the top of the stairs through the large window there I could see the moon was almost full. I stood staring at it for a long time, fatigue moving over my muscles but a hunger deep in the pit of my stomach. Not seeing Ellie for several nights wasn't sitting right with me. Knowing that Matt had touched her as I now wanted to was clawing at my gut, making me sick. The image of his tongue on her skin, his arms around her, him so much as speaking her name pissed me off. Before I knew what I was really doing, I was across the courtyard in the back of the house and shifting, my only drive, my only intent was to get to Ellie. To see her, to smell her. I shifted and my wolf rejoiced in feeling the freedom of the dirt under our paws as I galloped toward Ellie's house. The wind howled in my ears and my heart was racing, a sense of terror of not seeing her for several days drove me faster through the moonlight to the woods that led to her. I knew these woods well, I had spent almost all of my childhood in them until I began shifting. Then I began exploring even farther out. I breached the hill out of the woods and saw Ellie's lights were still on in her room. There was a feeling in my chest I couldn't stop and I threw my head back and howled, releasing all of my emotions into the call. I waited only a moment and then saw her silhouette in the window. She moved the curtain aside and we stared at each other only a moment before I began running across the field to her.

Ellie

I paced beside my bed. I hadn't heard from Bryce, Matt or Arick. Had they discovered anything? Was anything different? Why was he ignoring me suddenly? Wade and Tessa had gone to bed in their rooms hours ago but I couldn't sleep. I had tossed back and forth in bed and then resorted to pacing. I heard a howl on the hill out in the field. I moved to the curtain as fast as I could, almost ripping the curtain off the rod. It was Bryce, I saw his black wolf standing proud on that hill. I turned from the window and raced downstairs, careful to keep my steps light so as not to disturb anyone.

Bryce reached the porch just as I opened the door and he walked in like he lived here, which made me smile. He stayed as a wolf until he was upstairs in my room and then shifted. My hungry eyes soaked in every muscle as it appeared from the black fur. "Bryce, what hap-" His hand clamped over my mouth as he stared into my eyes. "Not right now. I need you." Was all he said before he kissed me. Hard.

There was a need this time as he held me, laid me back on the bed and pressed me into the mattress with his weight. He lifted the hem of the oversize shirt I was wearing and moved my panties aside as he continued to kiss me. I was already wet for him, that's all I ever was around him. He slid his middle finger in me and I whimpered against his mouth, my arms tightening around his neck as he worked his magic with my body. I hadn't realized just how much I missed him, his warmth and him being near. He pulled his hand off me to lift my shirt higher until he could grab a nipple in his teeth. I cried out and lurched up against his mouth. But he clamped a hand over my mouth. "Shh." He said softly as he continued to assault my senses. I felt the same need he was showing, and I wasn't going to be patient. I bucked and it did nothing to move him. Finally, I pushed against his shoulders, and he rolled onto his back, bringing me with him. I kissed him, our tongues dancing as I straddled his hips and took him deep in me. I groaned at the feeling of stretching around him. He swallowed the noise and rolled me onto my back, where he took control of the rhythm, and it was slow and delicious, but I needed fast and hard. I wrapped my legs around his hips and urged him to go faster but then he stopped, just holding me close to his chest. He broke our kiss and rested his forehead against mine.

"Ellie, oh God. Ellie. I need you." He said as a breathless whisper. I opened my eyes and looked into his. There was pain there, but also desire and something much deeper that I didn't want to talk about. Staying in me, he rose up on his elbows to look at me and smooth my hair back from my face. "All those wasted years. I'm so sorry, Ellie. I never should have let you leave." Tears filled my eyes and a tear slipped back into my hair. I felt emotion tighten a knot in my chest and couldn't make my throat work to speak. My vision blurred and I felt tears start to slip from my eyes. "Oh no, God no. Please don't cry. I'm so sorry." He kissed me again and pulled out of me, reaching between our bodies to allow his thumb to coax desire back through my blood as he rubbed my clit. Tears were still falling from my eyes as I closed them. This was so different for Bryce, this show of emotion. It was amazing and made me feel drunk but my body still wanted him. I could feel it throbbing, waiting for him to come back inside, to shoot me into outer space like he'd already done so many times. I ran my hands through his hair and threw my head back, feeling my first orgasm begin low in my stomach. He didn't change his rhythm, he didn't stop what he was doing. He just kept pushing me higher and higher until my world shattered into a million stars. Before I floated down to Earth he was inside me again, this time not gentle but pushing me up the plain again to the peak. This time when I came, it was around his cock deep inside me and I cried out at the intense pleasure. He clasped his hand over my mouth before groaning quietly against my neck. I felt his orgasm rip through him and he tensed and then hot liquid was running down my leg to the bedsheet. I don't know how long we lay there, just floating together. Gentle caresses on shoulders, feathered kisses against skin. He slid off me and I went to my bathroom to get a towel and cleaned up. When I turned around, he was standing in the bathroom doorway, watching me. I stole a glance and saw he was messy and almost hard. He smiled at me and took the towel and wet it in the sink before cleaning himself up. He then took my hand and led me back to the bed where he took my t-shirt off. "Nothing between us, Ellie. Ever." I nodded, knowing what he was asking and then I let him pull me into bed and under the covers. He sat against the headboard and held me as he stroked my hair.

"That was . . . intense." I said hesitantly.

I felt him swallow. "Yeah, it's been a rough day. Did I hurt you?"

I pulled away and looked at him in the moonlight. "No, not at all. But what happened?" I bit my lip, worried what he was about to tell me. "Is it about dad?"

He shook his head, not dropping my gaze. "No, it was just how Matt was so familiar with you and he kept goading me on. I should have known better."

I smiled at him then. "So, you rushed over here to pee on the bushes?"

He did laugh then, and some tension left his shoulders. "Something like that. But I did realize something."

"Oh boy, what in the world could Matt make you realize?" I kept my tone light and teasing but I was so nervous at the same time. This is where he would tell me that he didn't think we'd make sense and this was goodbye.

"I never want to be away from you, Ellie. I want you, just you. Forever." I glanced away, not ready for what he said next. "I want to mark you as mine." I swallowed before looking at him again.

"When we were kids," I said, not sure how to begin next. "You always had something better to do, something more fun to see. And I can't help but think there's another woman out there for you." I was having trouble getting the words out around the knot in my throat. I didn't want to think about him with another woman but knew that was possible. Bryce grasped my chin and made me look at him. "I have no idea how the fuck we are not mates. But no one, and I mean no one, will ever make me smile with smart ass answers like you. Will never surprise me with how tough you are, can't begin to impress me with what they know about engines. Whoever might be out there will never know my past like you do. You are it for me, Ellie. The end of the road."

I lowered my eyes and blinked several times, not sure how to respond. "You made it so incredibly easy to fall for you, Ellie. You try so hard to have a rough exterior, only to hide this soft side you want to keep from everyone. But I've seen it, I saw it when we were kids and when you were with Megan the other night. I don't want to go on in a world where you are not with me." I told myself I wouldn't cry, and was begging myself not to cry. To not crack. I had stalled enough that he released a breath. "Don't answer me right this minute. Just promise me you'll think about it." His words kept echoing in my head even as silence fell between us. "I will think about it." I promised.

"I can deal with that. For now." He pulled me close to his chest again. "I'm going to stay until you fall asleep and then I have to get back to the pack house."

I frowned. "Why can't you stay?" The disappointment in my voice was very evident to me, but I had hoped he didn't pick up on it.

"Matt wants me to show some of his wolves the ropes. Damon is going to come guard you the next few nights while I teach them the territory." His arm gripped me tighter.

"So I won't get to see you for how long?" I didn't like that idea at all. Bryce being around kept me feeling safe and rooted in the here and now instead of getting into trouble trying to find dad.

"Just a few nights. Until I can bring the Cielo pack up to speed. They're also going to help look for your father. But Matt is keeping tabs on us and until I'm sure he can be trusted I can't let him think you mean more to me than he thinks." His thumb was rubbing the very edge of my shoulder and that was making me sleepy. His words made sense, but I knew I was going to miss him. And that was the last thought I had before I fell into blissful sleep.

Chapter Twelve

Ellie

The next few days flew by helping Wade get settled in and learn the different places around our small town. It was a lot of fun watching females stammering as he tried to treat them or their family. Word was out that a new doctor was in town helping Dr. Savoy. So far, no one had asked where dad was. I wanted to keep it under wraps for now, waiting for something to circulate that hadn't been shared and then maybe there would be another lead. I hadn't heard from Bryce since the night I fell asleep in his arms. No texts, no late-night stalks from the hill. I had been watching. I didn't want to admit to myself or him that I was irked. He said repeatedly that I was it, that he couldn't be without me and now radio silence?

I stared at my phone now, looking at Megan's text to make sure I was still coming to help decorate for her party, which was the next night. A smile curved my lips as I answered her quickly and changed my clothes. Mid-afternoon sun shone through my window as I dug through my clothes and found the tight leather pants that I knew would drive Bryce crazy. I was sure he'd either see me or hear about me being there. And I wanted him to want me as much as I wanted him. I found a white t-shirt that was too tight across the bust and wore my push-up bra so my cleavage was peeking out of the deep V of the neck of the shirt.

I pulled on my leather jacket and grabbed my helmet from the hook as I left the room. I found the fob Bryce had been talking about in the center console of my car and then climbed on my motorcycle and let the engine purr under me for a moment before kicking up gravel to travel the short distance to the pack house.

As I approached the pack house, I clicked the fob and the gate swung open and the guard at the stand gave me a wave with a smile. I nodded in return and went up the large circular driveway. I saw Matt's entourage was parked in the front, several men standing outside with their hands clasped in front of them, their stern expressions begging someone to mess with them. Not much had changed with ol' Matt.

I left my helmet with the bike and removed my gloves and unzipped my jacket as I climbed the front steps to the house. The door opened before I could raise my hand to the bell and the maid greeted me with a smile. Megan was running down the stairs to greet me, trying not to show her excitement as only an-almost teenager could. "Thanks for the help. The decorator is here, asking me all kinds of questions. Daddy left me in charge, and I can't make any decisions because I want everything to be perfect." She tucked a tuft of hair behind her ear as she looked around the entrance. "Dad invited Matt to my party and he's so dreamy." I only nodded and smiled at her girlish crush. I had said that about Bryce more than once at her age. Megan didn't miss a beat and kept going. "The party is going to be pink and gold, but they keep asking me questions and

I wanted another woman's perspective. Have you had a shift party before, Ellie?"

I wrinkled my nose at her. "No, I was a tomboy. And my dad and brother didn't really know about girl's birthday parties." Megan frowned at me. "No mom?" I shook my head with a sad smile. "She took off after I was born. I have no idea where she is." Megan's eyes lowered and I rushed on. "It was okay, my brother and dad were great. I miss them."

"I'm sorry about your family. I know it's hard without all of them near." Her fingers went to the gold locket around her neck, and she looked away for a minute before forcing a smile for me and taking my hand. "Come on, this fru-fru decorator is back here. No doubt losing his mind because I took off."

I followed her. The dining hall was now decorated with pink and gold balloons and runners, curtains of lights were hung in each doorway, twinkling in soft white lights. The party was going to be at night at the peak of the Hunter's moon for Megan to shift. The young girl led us out onto the patio where it was decorated like a grand ball. Ice sculptures of wolves and birds and butterflies were going to be displayed, she explained. All of them back lit. More curtains of lights lined the patio to create an intimate ambiance. The mid-afternoon light didn't hide how beautiful it was all going to be once it was lit. "I think it looks okay," Megan was saying now. "But does it look great?" She was obviously worried as she chewed her lip while surveying.

"Well," I said, not sure I knew much more than she did. "You want it to look nice, but you're going to be the star of the show.

So do you want people to be staring at the decorations or you?" I looked at her now.

"True. But I want it to be memorable for everyone, including me." She was still worrying her bottom lip. "I don't think you have anything to worry about." I patted her shoulder in reassurance. "Did you pick out what you're wearing?"

"Yes, I did . . ." She trailed off.

"What's wrong?" I asked, trying to catch her gaze.

She sighed. "It's my 12th birthday. I had hoped my entire life I'd have a step-mother to help me get ready. But it's just me." I pulled her close. I knew similar pain. "I could come help you get ready. I'm not your mom or stepmother, but you can think of me as a crazy aunt."

Megan squeezed me tight. "I was so hoping you'd say that! But I didn't want to make you uncomfortable. Thank you!"

I looked around the patio now. The decorator company was still putting up balloons and a woman was struggling with the ladder behind us. I stepped over to steady the ladder and she smiled kindly at me over her shoulder. "Thank you. I'm terrified to go up there."

"Heights?" I guessed.

She cast her brown gaze up to where a balloon wasn't secured. "Yes, Ma'am."

"No worries, I'll get it." I went up the ladder and had to stretch up on my tiptoes to reach. I leaned across the top of the ladder, bent slightly at the waist as I tried to reach where the balloon needed to be secured to the ribbon hanging loose.

"What the fu—" I heard before big hands grasped my hips and yanked me down. I yelped in surprise and kicked the ladder away so I didn't get my ankle caught on the steps. The next moment I was against a hard chest, surrounded by a familiar scent and definitely a boner pressed against my leather-clad ass.

"What the fuck do you think you're doing?!" Bryce demanded now, not releasing me.

I looked over my shoulder at him. "I'm playing with latex balls to set up for Megan's party. What are you doing?" I challenged, looking down and motioning with my chin to the hard-on that was growing by the second.

"What I'm not doing is getting ogled by a visiting alpha, that's for sure."

"Oh, relax. No one even saw me here." I pushed at his abs behind me until he let me go and faced him then. My chest was heaving with the adrenaline of being pulled off the ladder, because of his scent and because this was the first time in days I had seen him and he was giving me the third degree?

The decorator cleared her throat and stepped forward. "I apologize, Beta. I was scared of the height and Luna went up there before I could stop her."

"Not Luna," I said and that made the woman even more confused by his reaction.

Megan giggled then. "Uncle Bryce, why are you so mad? Are you worried she'll fall?"

"Besides the point-" he cut himself off. "Excuse us a minute, Megan. Please."

Bryce grabbed my hand and dragged me into the house, down the long hallway to his office, where I had heard Grayson talking about my family and he shoved me into his office and I heard the door slam behind me and the lock click. In the next moment, Bryce grabbed my wrist again and spun me around and I was pressed against the wall with his hands all over me. His face was pressed into my neck as his thumbs moved back and forth across my nipples.

"You're in heat, Ellie." He said breathlessly as he pushed into me, our clothes and my ridiculously tight pants between us. But he was hard and I could feel him throbbing. Or was that me throbbing?

"That pompous alpha was staring at your ass stretched in that fucking leather you had to wear today. I can't stand the thought of anyone touching you. Anyone else making you scream." As he talked he moved my pants down my legs and I didn't want to stop him. I kicked the pants off and he lifted me as if I weighed nothing and took me to the couch where he sat down with my legs on either side of his waist, exposing my heat to him. He licked his middle finger and shoved it in me easily. I cried out and grasped his shoulders, already feeling that delicious pressure build. It wasn't long before I was panting and grinding against his hand, aching in that deep part of me. As his finger moved in me, his thumb moved over my clit and he watched his hand working on me. I threw my head back and moved against his hand faster. "You're so fucking beautiful, Ellie. And mine." He slowed his motions and I felt his gaze on me. "Say it." He said to me when I looked at him "Say you're mine."

I nodded. "Only yours, Bryce. Always." I kissed him then and he picked up the tempo with his hand and I came quickly, my scream absorbed by his kiss. He buried his hand in my hair and held me close for his kiss as he deepened it and it felt different than the others. This felt like love. He held me for a long time after, placing kisses on any skin he could reach.

I was sitting astride his lap, his hand in my hair and I was holding onto his arms with my hands. He looked at me for what seemed like a long time. "Ellie, I-" I held my breath, almost knowing what he was going to say next. "I've fallen so hard for you." He said and dropped his hands. "You're so fucking amazing and strong. I don't understand how I didn't see it before. And I know you're going through a lot right now and there's still a lot of things we need to talk through, but . . . you deserve to know how much you mean to me."

I wrapped my arms around his shoulders and held him close. He pulled me close and rested his hand against my neck. I wasn't ready to let down that last wall between Bryce and what part of my heart he didn't already have.

I don't know how long we sat in each other's embrace before he stood with me in his arms. My legs fell toward the floor but because of the way he was holding me, they dangled above the floor. "I have something for you upstairs." He said before a peck of a kiss on my lips before setting me on my feet. I walked over to my leather pants and pulled them on and then my shoes. "I think you already gave me some of it," I teased as I fastened my pants. He laughed then and took my hand – not my wrist – and led me upstairs to his room. I'd been here before when he brought me while I was unconscious, but I hadn't seen it fully. It was very shades of forest green and wood accents. Very masculine in appearance yet somehow cozy. The room was big enough to be a suite, with a long table at the window to my left under the window and books lining the wall on the other side. Like a study with a bed, I realized. And it all smelled like him. I drank it in and took a deep inhale of the scent of this room and of him.

Bryce let go of my hand, turned to me and smiled. "Close your eyes." I looked at him suspiciously and did as he told me to. While I waited patiently, I heard him open the closet door and I could only imagine what he was pulling out.

I heard rustling of plastic and then it was quiet for a moment. He took both my hands and led me deeper in the room. He turned me by my shoulders ever so slightly before stepping away.

"Okay," he said. "Open your eyes."

On his bed he had laid out the sexiest black dress I had ever seen. It was a sequined spaghetti strap with blush rhinestone accents on the straps and long the low neckline. Beside it were blush pink heels and a clutch to match the shoes. Makeup had been chosen as well. A long, black jeweler's box laid on top of the dress. I looked up at him with my eyebrows raised. He opened the box and took out a diamond tennis bracelet that he clasped on my wrist. It fit perfectly.

"It's beautiful." I smiled at him.

"You are the most beautiful woman in the world. And I want you to shine as bright as the diamond you are." This side of Bryce was so new I didn't know what to say or think. I felt my eyes fill with tears.

"Oh, baby. Don't cry." He pulled me close. He smoothed my hair as he shushed me quietly. "Do you not like it? Are the colors wrong?"

I shook my head and sniffed. "It's incredibly thoughtful, Bryce. Thank you."

"But you don't like it?" He was really worried I wouldn't like it? Crack. The first crack in the wall I had left.

"I love it! It's just so much. A lot has happened in the last few weeks and I guess it all just caught up with me. I haven't slept well and the phone at the house keeps going off at all hours of the night because of Wade being the doctor now." I giggled and wiped my tears away and stood away from Bryce. "I think there's too many females that don't have a problem and just keep calling to talk to Wade." I picked up the dress and held it to my chest tightly before comparing it to my size. It would fit perfectly. "I'll save you the first dance," I said, smiling at him.

"Oh no," he said, a playful smile cracking across his face. "You'll save them all for me, brat." He cupped my cheek. "I'd love to see you in it so I can figure out how I'm going to get you out of it."

"Oh no," I returned just as playfully. "You're going to get your first glimpse tomorrow night. Megan invited me to help her get ready so she and I can get ready together."

He looked disappointed but nodded his acceptance. "She picked out your makeup, some of that stuff I couldn't even begin to spell, let alone know what color to get. I hope you don't mind. You didn't have a lot of makeup at your place." He was babbling and it was cute to see him nervous. Finally, he just stopped and ran a hand through his hair. "I just want you to feel comfortable here, Ellie. I want to mark you and have you come live with me."

I put the dress on his bed and sat down. I hadn't really thought about what us being together would mean for our living situation. I hadn't thought of ever being with Bryce and what that would mean long term. I chewed my bottom lip before answering. "My garage is at Dad's. I'd have to go there every day, anyway." I didn't really know what I was implying. Part of me wanted this to slow down, another part of me wanted to go get my stuff now and be with Bryce.

Bryce nodded and hooked his thumbs in his jean pockets. "I understand. We don't have to talk about it now. There's a lot going on in the world we need to get through first." He motioned to the bedroom door with his head, but I could hear the disappointment in his voice. I don't know why I couldn't just throw myself into his arms and yell "yes!" but I was genuinely concerned he would find his mate and leave me devastated. I couldn't move past that fear. Having lost Tanner early in life, losing Bryce would hurt at least that much, probably more. It was a pain I don't think I could come back from.

I stood now and walked past Bryce, my intention to go back to Megan. He grabbed my wrist and pulled me to him. "We will talk about this, Ellie. I was a fucking idiot to let you leave ten years ago. I will not make the same mistake again."

I nodded and offered no other resistance. He pulled me close and kissed me, moaning into the kiss as I deepened it holding onto him. There was a knock at his bedroom door and Arick opened the door. "Oh, sorry." He said and I had never seen him look so shocked and embarrassed. He had to have known about Bryce and I but I don't think he had confirmation. "Ellie," he said by way of greeting, but didn't move from the doorway. "Alpha," I responded, not willing to meet his eyes. My face was bright red and I was hiding my cheek against Bryce's chest. He held me close as he waited for what Arick needed. "Dad wants to see us downstairs." Arick said before backing out of the room. I stiffened at the thought of coming face to face with Grayson again. He wasn't my biggest fan and I couldn't understand why. I had to admit he was right, nothing but trouble followed my family. Mom had run off, my brother had been murdered and now dad was missing.

"It's okay," Bryce said, smoothing his hands down my arms. "We found out Navarro hired the bastard that broke into your house. So Cielo and Shadow Wolf may be going to war against Diablo pack before long."

I sank onto his bed and wrapped my arms around my middle as my blood ran cold. "There's no link between Diablo and my father. Could this be connected to Tanner somehow?"

"I don't know," Bryce answered me, his voice as grim as my thoughts. War between 3 packs spelled death for many wolves and every pack was vulnerable with all the pregnant wolves. This was not going to end well, but I kept going back to what was prompting all of this. The packs had been peaceful for generations. What the hell was going on? "I feel like I'm in a twilight zone right now."

"I know, it's rough to take it all in." He looked at the door. "I have to go talk to them, will you be all right here?" I nodded. "Yeah, I'm going to help Megan finish setting up and then we have to pick out her hair and makeup." He looked sad for having to leave me, but he turned and left the room without another word, the door clicking shut quietly behind him.

I don't know how long I sat there, my mind racing with scenarios about this latest news. There was something I was missing, but I didn't know what. I shook it off and went to go find Megan. She would get to have a special day, at least.

We spent the rest of the day running through hairstyles and makeup colors and trying out what worked best for her in each light before settling on what she would wear.

I was boxing up the makeup she wouldn't be using when her voice cracked as she asked me "does it hurt?"

I looked at her, closing a tube of mascara. "Your first shift?" I asked hesitantly.

She nodded, her dark eyes wide with worry. I was quiet for a moment as I considered the best way to answer such a delicate question "It's different for everyone. Mine wasn't very painful but some of my friends said there was a lot of pain, but that it only lasted a few seconds. Kind of like cracking your knuckles because your bones all change."

Megan looked at her hands in her lap. "I've been too scared to ask anyone. But I don't know what to expect after. How do you change back and forth?"

I sat beside her on her bed and put my arm around her shoulder, searching my memory for the times I've shifted. "Well, once the moonlight hits your skin, you'll feel a tingle. Then you sort of picture the wolf hair coming through your skin and then envision running across a field on 4 legs." Megan was looking at me intensely now and I kept going. "Once you shift, you don't have your clothes. So, you have to take them with you or plan where you'll shift back. Changing back is as easy as remembering what it's like to stand on two legs. That time can feel weird, and you might feel some back pain for a little bit, depending on how long you're a wolf. But it's so wonderful running as a wolf. I can't even describe it." I know I sounded wistful, but I figured it would help Megan feel more comfortable if she knew how much I enjoyed my own shifting and being my own wolf. "You gain energy from the ground beneath your paws. Does your dad have wolves that will run with you when you shift?"

Megan nodded. "Yes, they ran with him when he shifted the first time. And they'll have the help to bring me clothes before I shift back. But I'm just so nervous to shift."

"Your mother sat with me when I had my first shift since my mother wasn't there. She wasn't much older than I was, but she was an incredible woman. And her blood lives on in you. I'm sure she will be with you in spirit and help guide you."

I glanced at the clock by her bed. "Now, it's late and while you're so beautiful you don't need beauty sleep, you do need some rest. Tomorrow is a big day." Megan climbed into her bed and I pulled the covers up and kissed her forehead. "Thanks for letting me help you today."

Megan smiled at me. "Thanks for being here. It means a lot to Dad and me."

As I turned her lights off and left the room, I realized I hadn't really talked to Arick since I'd been back. I stopped at Bryce's room, realizing I was starting to feel at home and my dress was still on the bed from earlier. I moved to pick it up, not sure how I was going to get it home on my bike because I hadn't brought my pack when I realized the shower was running. I smiled a little to myself and hung the dress up and sat the makeup on the table beside the bed, fully intending to join Bryce and enjoy his shower. I took my shirt off and started working on the hook behind my back when a woman gasped, wearing only a towel as she emerged from the bathroom. "Oh, I didn't know we weren't alone." Her dark hair was wet and falling around her shoulders. Her red lips were large and pouty. She was tall, brunette and rail thin. Everything I was not. "I'm Mitzy," she smiled at me. Completely comfortable in Bryce's room, I realized. "I thought we were alone, but a third is always a good thing." She was still smiling as she looked at me from head to toe. Tears flooded my vision, and I took a deep breath as I put my shirt back on. "No, it was my mistake. Wrong room, I guess." I stormed out, leaving her there with her mouth open and all but ran downstairs. I heard someone yell my name, but I was too close to losing it to stop. I just kept going, stopping only long enough to unclasp the bracelet he'd given me and throw it toward the doorstep of the house. I left my helmet on the back of the bike and took off into the dark night as fast as I could, picturing Bryce and that brunette together. He must have been in the shower with her, because she had thought they were alone. How could I have been so stupid? I should have known better. I was old baggage to keep in the closet until something better came along. Fuck, for all I knew he had found his mate since lunch.

I knew I was crying and the cool night air dried my tears as I sped back to my father's house. Shame burned the back of my throat as I locked my bike up in the garage and went into the kitchen, avoiding my aunt, not caring where Wade was. I just needed quiet and to be alone. I turned off every light in my room, locked my bedroom door and went to shower. As I stood under the hot water, my knees buckled, and I fell to the floor sobbing deep from my soul. I hadn't wanted to admit it, but I had started to love Bryce. The idea of having someone that wouldn't leave me that wanted me around. Someone who wouldn't just disappear on me.

The last thought sobered me up. All this time we had been working with the assumption he didn't want to be taken – but what if Dad had left because he just had had enough of being pack doctor? This new thought sent new waves of pain over me. I don't know how long I sat there crying. I only know I got to a point where there was nothing left. So I shut the water off and left the bathroom. On the table by the bed, my phone was buzzing. I saw Bryce's name. I ignored the call and saw I already had twenty-two missed calls from him, sixteen text messages begging me to answer the phone. I couldn't stand it anymore and I powered the phone down and climbed into bed, not bothering to dry off. I just closed my eyes and did my best to forget everything.

Chapter Thirteen

Bryce

Grayson's words were echoing in my head as I climbed the stairs. He was a pompous ass and he didn't know what he was talking about. "Get rid of her, Arick. Banish her from the pack. That entire family is nothing but trouble." Grayson had started the conversation advising Arick he had set up time with the Navarro alpha to talk about what was going on. Arick and I had both acknowledged that the Alpha may not know about Ellie's father and the thug that had broken into her house. But whatever was going on it was deep.

I opened my bedroom door, frowning in the darkness but then I saw a frame under the covers and realized Ellie had stayed the night. Thankful, I quickly began stripping my clothes off and sat on the bed to take off my boots, letting my mind push aside the night's discussion. I just needed Ellie's warmth now. As I reached for the laces of my boots, long, thin, gangly arms wrapped around my shoulders and tiny tits were mashed against my back. I jumped off the bed and flicked on the lights. Missy or Susie or whatever-the-fuck-her name was sitting naked in my bed. She'd been here before, so security might have let her back in. But-

"Bryce, it's been a long time." She purred at me, stretching naked on the bed on her side. I felt repulsed at the sight of her tiny and flat body. It wasn't full and curvaceous like Ellie's. It hadn't filled my hands the way Ellie's does now. "I thought we had someone else here with us. She was here when I got out of the shower. Do you have a new play thing?"

I frowned and looked around the room. The dress wasn't laid on the bed anymore, but the makeup was on a side table. "Who let you in?"

"Alpha brought me here. He said you'd been lonely." She sat up on her knees, quickly as a pout pulled at her bottom lip. "And you know I missed you. We had some good times." My mind was racing, I couldn't process it all until I replayed her words. She was trailing a single long red fingernail down my chest. I grabbed her wrist and held her away from me. "What do you mean another woman was here?" My heart was racing as I waited for her response, but somehow I already knew what she was going to say.

"Some blonde chick. Big tits, black and white wolf tattoo on her back. She was pretty upset." Whatshername threw her head back and laughed. "I was kind of disappointed, she looked like a lot of fun."

Now I was pissed. This couldn't have looked good and the fact she didn't confront me and had likely left had my blood boiling. "I don't have any fucking clue what's going on. But I want you out. Now."

She pulled her wrist away and rubbed it, that ugly pout on her face again. "Don't be like that. We had a lot of fun. We still could-
"

"I have a mate now. So get out."

She moved closer to me and I smelled her loud as hell perfume. "Mated or not, you know your way around a woman. I remember that well. I can make you feel good, too." She half purred.

"You won't get the chance. Now, get. Out." I brushed past her, hitting her in the shoulder as I walked by and hit the intercom button by the bed. "Security. Get in here now."

Her mouth dropped open and she covered her tits with her arms. "You can't be serious, Bryce"

"As a heart attack." Before I finished my sentence, the door flung up and guards came rushing in. "The lady here," I used the word ironically. "Was just leaving. See to it she never comes back." The guards knew the protocol and she was yelling and screaming as they drug her away by her arms. Arick walked around the corner, rubbing his head and looking very confused. "What was that about?" He asked.

Arick was the last person I wanted to see right now. "That's some bitch you let in here and I think Ellie might have found her in my room."

Arick's mouth dropped open. "I didn't let her in. I've been here all day."

Now I frowned, but I was already dialing Ellie's number on my cell. No answer. I dialed again.

I sank to the bed and rested my forehead on my hands, not sure what to do. I didn't care how it had happened; I needed a plan to make it right. I tried several more times and sent her text messages asking her to listen. "What the fuck am I going to do?" I heard myself ask, my chest so tight it felt like I'd never have a deep breath again.

"You really love her, don't you?" Arick smirked as he folded his arms across his chest and leaned against the doorframe.

"I can't believe I was so stupid before and let her leave ten years ago. It's like a missing part of myself. I don't know how we're not mates." My voice cracked as I finished the sentence. I saw Arick nodding and looking down. "It was like that with Sarah. How do you know you're not mates? She's only been back a few weeks."

"I haven't felt that pull you described. And I tried to link to her human mind while I was a wolf. It didn't work." I was ready to start crying. I needed her here, I needed to feel her. I needed to know she was okay. But I was sure her heart was shattered, and I had no idea how to begin to put it back together.

"You know," Arick was saying now, walking over to the window and looking up at the full moon. "You're mated the first full moon after her 18th birthday."

"Yes, I know. I would have felt it. What does it matter? I don't care who my mate is, Ellie is it for me." I was growing frustrated with his riddles, and I was trying to decide if I go kick her door in or not. I dialed her number again, it only rang three times and went to voicemail. She was ignoring my calls. "Only if you're together on that full moon." Was Arick's only response, not looking away from the window.

Realization crashed through my brain. She could still be my mate, but we hadn't shared a full moon since she had turned 18. But as angry as she was right now, she could still reject me and that put me back at square one.

I had to go to her, something was pulling at me but as I tried to move past Arick, he turned and put a hand on my shoulder, stopping me. "I understand how you're feeling, but we cannot do this with another pack here. It looks bad and she needs time to cool off before it escalates."

Anger swelled and tightened my chest. He was right, fuck it to hell. "She's not coming back if I don't go after her." *Fuck*. My voice cracked. The thought of never seeing her again was going to be my undoing.

"Perhaps she can calm down enough to still come to the party tomorrow night." Arick offered with a squeeze of my shoulder. "Megan talked about her non-stop at dinner. I'm so glad she has a female in her life now that Ellie is back in town. I'm sure she can convince Ellie to still come to the party." Arick was so quiet and calm I wanted to punch something, *anything*.

"I can, uncle Bryce!" Megan said as she came around the corner, rubbing her eyes against the light. "How mad is she?"

"Uh, well. . . " I searched for the right words. "She's pretty mad. I don't know what to do. And why are you up?" I tried to sound stern, but fear was keeping me from doing much wholeheartedly. She heaved a dramatic sigh. "The woman being thrown out was screaming. *A lot*. It would wake the dead, easily."

"Yeah, you have your dad to thank for that." I flopped back on the bed, trying to calm down. I couldn't lose Ellie now.

"I had nothing to do with Mitzy being here tonight. Why do you think I did?" Arick turned to look at me now. I glared at him. "She said the Alpha brought her here."

Arick frowned and shook his head. "I didn't let anyone in." He went to the receiver and picked up the phone. "The woman that was just removed, who did she arrive with?" After an eternity, he simply muttered "I see," before replacing the phone on the cradle.

"What?" I sat up and forward, wanting to know what was going on.

"She was with my father when he came in. But he left without her."

Megan glanced up. "The way she was screaming, I don't blame him. Uncle Bryce, is Ellie's dress still here? And the makeup or did she take it with her?"

I nodded at the table on the other side of the bed. "She left the makeup." I walked to the closet. "And someone hung up the dress."

"Okay, give me the dress. I just sent her a distress message that I made up and she should be here tomorrow. But she can't see you. So disappear when she gets here. I'll let you know the time." She took the dress from me, swiped the makeup from the table and left the room. If this worked like she wanted it to, I really owed that kid. And I made a note to not underestimate her moving forward.

"I take gift cards, by the way!" She called down the hall before she kicked her door shut. Arick laughed then. "Gotta love that kid." He said with pride in his voice. I nodded. I was sure if anyone could get her here tomorrow it was Megan. But there was still a small chance it wouldn't work. Looking at the dial on the table in front of the window, I saw the full moon wouldn't peak until almost 10pm the next night. It could take that long for our mate bond to activate. I was going to lose my mind before then, wondering if this was it. If I could finally have Ellie as my own.

I sighed and scrubbed my face. Arick kind of laughed. "It's so funny to see you so torn up after all the women you couldn't even remember their names." He paused a moment, glancing down for a moment before saying, "Don't mess this one up, Bryce. She's special." He left the room then, and I was alone with my thoughts. My hopes are up now. She could still be my mate. I started rapid-firing texts to her, trying to get her to listen to me, but there was no response and finally I gave up and went on patrol, needing to clear my head. But as usual, I found myself on the hill behind her house. My wolf whimpered as we laid in the moonlight, wishing she would come to the window.

This was going to be the longest 24 hours of my life.

Ellie

The bright morning sun shone through the window in my room. I didn't remember falling asleep. I cracked one eye open and looked at the clock on the wall. It was almost noon. So it wasn't morning sun. Then everything last night came rushing back and pain rushed through my chest and threatened to strangle me. Tears stung at my eyes and I shut them tightly and willed them away. I didn't want to face this today. Didn't want to think about the night he spent with someone else. He hadn't come for me, which I was grateful for. But also disappointed. How dare he string me along and then leave me hanging?

With a heavy sigh, I turned my phone on and threw it on the pillow next to my head as it started. I heard shuffling downstairs and knew that my aunt was doing things, but I just didn't feel like seeing anyone or anything. My phone began rapid buzzing and I reached for it. I had slept through the barrage of buzzing, apparently. Twenty seven text messages.

Bryce: *It's not what you think.*

Bryce: *She's been banned from the property.*

Bryce: *She came in with Grayson, I didn't even know she was here.*

Bryce: *I don't know what I can say to make this better.*

Bryce: *See what time it is? I'm up pacing the floor, missing you.*

Bryce: *Miss you.*

Bryce: *This place is so cold without you.*

Bryce: *I'd give anything to be with you right now.*

Bryce: *I miss you, Ellie.*

Bryce: *Please say something.*

Bryce: *Please let me know you got home safely. You were riding upset.*

Bryce: *Please, Ellie. Talk to me.*

Bryce: *This is me. You know what you mean to me.*

Bryce: *I love you, Ellie. I will do whatever it takes to make this up to you.*

With a snort, I closed his thread without reading the rest and checked other messages. There was a long message from Megan.

Megan: *I'm so nervous about my shift tomorrow. I can't wait to see you. I hope you're still coming. I really need you here.*

I threw the phone on the covers and flopped back on the bed. I was planning to skip the party all together so I didn't have to see Bryce with his other mistress.

My phone chirped two more times. I grabbed it and saw several more messages from Megan.

Megan: *I'm ordering lunch and when it gets here, I'm going to start getting ready. Can I order you something?*

Megan: *I let Uncle Bryce know how mad I am at him. I got the dress from his room and you don't have to see him. He's going to be out on hunts all day and will go down before we do. You're safe here. Please come over.*

I sighed. This kid was good. But I trusted her that I didn't have to see Bryce. So, I sent her a quick text letting her know I'd be over in thirty minutes and pulled on some jeans, a black t-shirt and ran a brush through my mangled hair and curled the ends really fast. Some mascara to make my eyes look normal and I was ready to go. I looked like I had been crying all night. But makeup would fix it later.

This time I took my car to the pack house. Valets were setting up out front, ready to park guest's cars as they came in. I handed him my key and thanked him as I went up the steps to the front door. Megan threw the door open, her hair in jumbo curlers and her purple fuzzy robe cinched so tight I wasn't sure how she was breathing. She threw her arms around me and hugged me and I patted her back. When she pulled away, I saw she had tears in her eyes. I wiped them away with my thumb. "Hey, hey. No tears today. Only happiness." I said softly.

"I was just so worried you weren't coming, and I had to go through this alone." She sniffed and then hooked her arm in mine and led me in the house and up the stairs to her room. Once there, I saw our dresses hung side by side on the canopy of her bed. The makeup was all laid out and her jewelry shimmered in the light on the table by her window. She closed the door behind us and sighed.

"I saw you leaving last night.. Then Uncle Bryce went to his room and a few minutes later security rushed in and this screaming banshee was pulled out and down the stairs. Then I went to Uncle Bryce's room. He was really upset." I didn't say anything, I just took off my jacket. "She was certainly at home there." Was all I said because my blood was beginning to boil.

"I've seen her around before. Not just with Uncle Bryce. She's been with most of the pack. It's really gross." Megan said on a fake gag. I smiled a little. "Uncle Bryce loves you very much and he wanted to go to you last night but Dad told him to hold off and let you calm down." That was probably the best advice, I acknowledged to myself. Because I would have gone for blood if he had come around last night. "Okay, enough about your uncle. Let's get me beautiful and you dressed!"

The next few hours were spent on hair and makeup with only a break to nibble at the lunch Megan had ordered. We shared a lot of laughs and were really bonding. It felt like just a few moments had gone by when the sun was sinking in the sky and the lights from the patio glowed into Megan's window. I looked out and down. It was beautiful with the pink and gold balloons and walls of curtain lights. Tables had been added and food and drinks were out. Champagne for the adults and punch for the kids. A few people had already arrived. I saw Matt talking to Arick on the steps that led off the patio to the pond. I watched as Bryce joined them and my breath caught. His hair was slicked back and his tux hugged every ridge, every muscle on his body. "Isn't he dreamy?" Megan said, seeing where I was staring. "Um, yeah." Was my feeble answer.

"I meant Matt. Eeww at Uncle Bryce and Dad." I looked at her then. "Speaking from experience, enjoy the view but don't touch. That's a hazardous object."

"Relax, he's not mate material. But he's really nice arm candy. And he's been incredibly charming while he's been staying with us."

I snorted and arched an eyebrow. I believed that. Everyone loved Matt. Except for me.. "Well, have fun either way. But buckle up, it's a bumpy ride." I said with a wink. That moment, Bryce turned and looked me dead in my eyes. He was clean shaven and his black hair being slicked back looked like him, but not him. His eyes pierced mine where I stood. He blew a kiss and a mock bow and I backed away from the window, not willing to acknowledge him. Even though Megan had explained Bryce had thrown Mitzy out, I was still raw from feeling betrayed.

I finished dressing. The spaghetti straps on the dress had turned out to be wrong for me, so I tucked them into the dress and the sweetheart neckline sat perfectly as a strapless. The gown slid to my ankles and the slit went up my left thigh to the very top. It felt naughty and indecent, but I loved it. Megan had a pair of black gloves I wore with it and I borrowed pink earrings to match my shoes. My silver hair was pulled up on my head in a smooth bun with tendrils curled near my temples. The makeup Megan had chosen for me were shades of silvers and pinks and I felt like Marilyn Monroe in this outfit. Megan's was like mine only pink with black accessories. We looked like we were a couple and we giggled at it.

"Well," Megan said as she smoothed a stray hair into her bun. "We know Uncle is down there and it's getting dark. We might as well get this over with." I smiled at her. "Did you want to walk down with your dad?" I asked, offering to go get him.

Megan answered a final text and sat her phone aside. "No, I want you to walk down with me. Please."

I pulled her hand into my elbow. "It would be my honor, my lady."

We giggled again and I had to admit that the total crap these last two weeks had brought me this kid to spend time with. And that was worth a lot. We looked at each other one last time, took a deep breath and started down the stairs together.

A hush fell over the crowd as we stepped out onto the patio and the crowd parted and I smiled for Megan as she beamed proudly. Arick walked forward and offered his arm. She took it with a smile only a little girl could give her father and the band began playing a soft melody and he led her to the dance space, and they started swaying. I stepped back into the crowd, watching the duo dance.

"Beautiful, isn't it?" Matt said beside me.

I smiled and nodded, leaning my head toward him as I watched other couples gather around Arick and Megan. The photographer that had been hired for the event was roaming and snapping pictures, not paying total attention to where he was going and he bumped into me and I fell against Matt. Thankfully he had been paying attention and caught me so I didn't fall and break my ankle in the sky high heels. "Are you all right?" He asked softly as he helped me gain my balance. "I'm fine. I wish I could blame the champagne, but I haven't had any yet. Just clumsy like usual." I laughed at my words, keeping my voice light. I heard growling in my head and I frowned, not sure where it was coming from. I searched the crowd and saw Bryce looking at me, murder in his eyes.

Bryce

I had been aware of Ellie being in the house since the moment she arrived. I knew she was upstairs with Megan getting ready. I prayed she would still wear the dress I had bought her.

EarlierI had sensed her watching me from somewhere and caught a glimpse of her in Megan's window. I was grateful she was watching me, her sexy stare burning a hole right through me. I was grateful she was even *willing* to look at me. Megan had been texting me updates throughout the day and some candid shots of Ellie in various states of ready, from wearing her "borrowed" satin robe I had also gotten her to her laughing at something Megan had said. The photos had lifted my spirits and I realized if this was all I would ever have of Ellie, I would live with it.

I had known the moment they had left the room; Megan had texted me. I had turned then, waiting and holding my breath to see her. And the vision that had greeted my hungry eyes had not disappointed. The dress's straps were nowhere in sight and the heart shaped neckline accentuated her larger form while embracing her slender waist and hugging her curvy hips. Her white toenails peeped out of the pink heels Megan had picked out for her to go with the black dress. My eyes lingered at her wrist, and I was saddened when I saw the bracelet wasn't there. She wore a single diamond teardrop necklace and pink earrings to match her shoes.

Arick walked forward and took Megan from Ellie's side and I was ashamed to admit I hadn't really noticed Megan at all. All I saw was Ellie. As Arick and Megan began the first dance, Ellie had melted into the crowd. The way she had at every party or event during our childhood.

I sat my champagne aside and started to make my way to her when Matt appeared beside her and she smiled, *she smiled,* at him. I clenched my jaw as I watched the two talk like old friends. The nerve in my temple was ticking and I definitely saw red. The photographer knocked into her and shoved her against Matt, who didn't hesitate to catch her and shoot me a look.

Ellie righted herself and laughed at something and I'd had enough. I walked over to her now, determined to get her away from the snake that had come into the pack.

I cleared my throat. "Alpha, Ellie promised me a dance. Would you mind terribly if I took her from you?" Before either of them could answer I pulled her close to me and we moved to the dance floor.

"That wasn't very smooth at all." Ellie commented, looking up at me and in the lighting Megan had carefully picked out she looked like a fairy princess in a magical forest.

"I wasn't worried about being smooth. I just wanted you away from him." I couldn't keep the snarl out of my voice.

She laughed lightly then and shook her head. "You're a fine one to be jealous. You just had a hot date last night."

I looked down into her eyes as we swayed to the music. "You don't believe I had anything to do with that, do you?" Her face sobered some. "I did at first," she lowered her eyes. "Megan told me you had her removed. But what happened before you had her removed?"

"Nothing, she was waiting for me when I got done with Arick and Grayson." I sighed and looked off into the distance. "I'm not embarrassed to admit I was comparing her to you and didn't even want to look at her again. So she's been banished from pack property, too. She couldn't return even if I wanted her to. Which I don't." I rushed on to explain. The music had changed, but I was still holding her in my arms and I wasn't ready to let her go.

Ellie nodded. "Megan said Grayson brought her?" She met my eyes to read my answer. "Yes, and I have no idea what he was thinking or why he left without her and I honestly don't care." I rested my head against hers. "You are the only woman welcome in my room or bed, Ellie. I swear to you."

She smiled sadly. "My heart was so broken, Bryce. This is what I was afraid of."

"I know, but we'll get through it. I promise. You just have to give me a chance." I then held my breath for her next words. She looked me in my eyes and said "I've loved you for at least one forever. I can't imagine myself without you, Bryce."

The band of anxiety that had been wrapped around my chest burst into a million shards and I wanted to scream from the roof of the pack house. Ellie Savoy was mine.

I pulled her against my body and kissed her like it was the first time. She wrapped her arms around my neck and lifted herself up to match me. I don't know how long we made out on the dance floor before Arick cleared his throat. "I'm cutting in before you do something these pups can't unsee." Ellie laughed and I smiled at the sound as it danced around me.

The rest of the night moved smoothly. Ellie was popular and spoke with so many people I lost count. She was a true lady through and through and I was so proud she allowed herself to be mine.

Chapter Fourteen

Ellie

It was nearing time for Megan to shift and my head was swimming from champagne, conversations with people I had just met, Bryce's hungry eyes on me and Arick stealing me for dances every chance he had. I felt at ease, I felt at home.

I saw the moon clear the clouds and went to gather Megan. "It's time, sweetheart." At the startled look on her face, I reached for her hand. "I've got you."

I led her to the clearing near the pond off to the east of the patio. I hugged her and smoothed her hair. "There is nothing to be afraid of. You will heal faster, run faster and be free. We've got you."

I let her step into the moonlight and still held her hand. The moonlight spilled onto her and I smiled at her and began twirling her like we were dancing as her fur began to shimmer in the blue light of the Hunter Moon. She cried out as her bones snapped for the first time as she moved to all fours. I grabbed her dress and she shook off in her wolf form and howled. The rest of the pack howled with her and the guards shifted quickly and they bound off into the woods as

Megan began her first moonlight run. I stood there for a moment and then stepped out into the moonlight and I felt something in me move. The world started to shift under my feet and I almost lost my balance. I searched the crowd for Bryce and then I felt it.

Mate. My wolf cried out for his.

Bryce was beside me the next moment, clasping my hand in his and leading me back to the house as I clutched Megan's dress tightly. This was so thrilling and so scary at the same time. I had read about the mate pull, but now I felt everything Bryce did, I was so in tune with him pulling me into the house and up the stairs and into his room, the images of what he was going to do to me running through both our minds until I didn't know where his consciousness stopped and mine started. . He kicked the door shut and turned the lock. Still not done, he cleared the table in front of the window where the blue moonlight spilled into his dark room and sat me on the desk before grasping my face and kissing me. His tongue danced with mine as he wedged his legs between mine where I sat on the desk. I don't know how long we kissed but I was completely drunk on this feeling of being bonded to Bryce.

He kissed down my neck. "Mine. Mate. Mine. Mate." He kept saying over and over again as he lifted the dress around my waist. I reached for his pants to undo his belt and zipper and took him in my hand and guided him to me where I was waiting for him. I was already wet and so ready for him I was dizzy. He began thrusting into me, bracing a hand against the glass behind me and all I could do was hold on for my life as he took us on a whirlwind. "Come for me, Ellie. Come for me, Mate." He ground against my ear and I did as he told me to, splintering into a million pieces as he kept thrusting in me. His release was nearing and he grabbed my ass to hold me still and I felt his teeth at the nape of my neck.

"Yes, Bryce, please." He bit me then, marking me as his. Another orgasm ripped through me and I was powerless to stop it and I screamed into his shoulder. He stiffened and held me close as he groaned out his release.

I was shaking from the power of being marked his, of being taken by my mate's body.

He was still wearing his tux jacket, his pants were around his ankles and my dress was up to my waist. I giggled as I realized we must look ridiculous. "What's so funny?" He asked breathlessly.

"Look at us, we must look like a wreck."

"Yeah, I suppose so." He started to leave my body, but we were locked together. I had heard dad explaining this to other females in the pack. Females would literally latch onto their males to ensure full mating and procreation of the next generation. I hadn't thought of it because I thought I didn't have a mate. But now when Bryce tried to leave my body, there was a painful pressure that caused me to whimper and wince.

He laughed now. "I guess you're stuck with me for tonight."

I wrapped my arms around his neck. "Sounds delicious to me." We were both laughing as he carried us to the bed. He kicked his pants off as he went and then laid me down gently before taking a box out of his jacket pocket and laying it beside my head and then removing his jacket and shirt. Then he climbed on the bed between my legs and sat back on his haunches and helped me shimmy out of my dress and took off the strapless bra and cast it aside.

Once we were completely nude, he rolled to his back and I laid on his chest astride him.

"What's in the box?" I asked, curious.

"Um, two things." He seemed hesitant to talk about it so of course now I was curious. I sat up with him still lodged deep inside me while he laid back against the pillow. I pulled the sheet of the bed around my bare breasts from his hungry gaze and I put a full stern look on my face. "What are you up to now?"

He made a hesitant face before asking, "Promise you won't be mad?"

"No." Was all I said. Moon only knew what he had planned, and I wanted to make sure I didn't promise him anything. Violence was always on the table.

He sighed and opened the box. The bracelet I had thrown back at the house was the first thing he pulled out. "You lost this last night and I'd like you to have it back." He clasped it around my right wrist instead of my left. I smiled at it as I ran a finger along the diamonds. "Why would I be mad about you being so thoughtful?"

"It's not that one you'll be mad at." He pulled out the next one and I stopped breathing. He snapped the box shut and threw it aside and the thud it made as it hit the carpet seemed to echo in my head. A beautiful marquis cut diamond on a band of white gold glinted at me in the moonlit room as it rested between his thumb and index finger. "I don't understand," I sounded breathless to myself, but that could be because of my heart pounding in my ears.

"Before I explain, I feel I should remind you that you're marked as mine now and I got this before I thought that would happen." He sounded really scared. "Are you mad?"

I blinked rapidly at the ring, not sure what I was feeling. He had planned to propose before we were mated? He took a deep breath and his arm unconsciously tightened around me. Through our links as mates, I could feel his anxiety as he began to explain. "We both thought I wouldn't be able to mark you as a mate, so I figured a ring made sense. I was planning on asking you tonight after Megan's shift. I had no idea we'd be mates. Arick said last night that mates are mated on the first full moon after their 18th birthday. But that you and I hadn't shared a full moon since you were fourteen. But I had already bought the ring when I bought the bracelet and I wanted the bracelet to warm you up to the idea of being reminded constantly that you're mine. And when you were settled in with that idea, I was going to ask you to be mine forever, mates or not. And then I decided to just bite the bullet and do it all tonight and-" He stopped and took a breath. "Please say something."

"I don't know what to say." The room was spinning and the corner of my vision blurred. But in the blur of all the emotions quickly changing in my thoughts, a sense of belonging and fulfillment began blooming deep in my chest.

"Then just . . . say yes." His voice was a quiet plea as he moved the ring closer to me.

Tears flooded my eyes as I started to nod. "Yes. I'll be yours forever."

He slid the ring on my finger and pulled me close. I cried against his neck for just a moment, more happy than I could have ever imagined. Then pushing up slightly, I looked in his eyes as he brushed my tears away. "From this day forward, you'll only cry happy tears because of me. I love you, Ellie. And I will spend the rest of my life showing you what you mean to me."

I broke again and started crying but he swallowed it up into a passionate kiss. His tongue invaded my mouth and I could feel him harden within me as it deepened to a heavy petting that made us both hungry for more. And it was still many more hours before we slept.

Chapter Fifteen

Bryce

The gray sky promised rain when I opened my eyes the next morning. Beside me, nestled under my arm was my mate.

My mate.

The words echoed in my ears as I thought of her that way. I still couldn't fathom how the moon had chosen her for me. She was so perfect as she slept soundly, small snores escaping her lips. I smoothed her hair back and touched her shoulder. At some point in the night, her body had released mine and it felt like a lifetime since I'd touched her, felt her skin on mine. The bond between us was strong and I felt myself tracing the bite mark on her shoulder where I had branded her as mine. She stirred then and I stilled, waiting for her to fall back asleep. But she inched away from me and looked up into my eyes, smiling a sweet smile. Satisfied with whatever she saw on my face, she yawned. "Morning," she said as she closed her eyes again and scooted as close to me as she could.

"How are you feeling?" I asked her, worried.

She stretched then and grimaced and looked at her shoulder toward the bite mark. "I'm sore in a lot of places." Her smile was still there, sweet and lazy. And then she yawed and curled up again at my side. "I'll shower in a bit and you can kiss all the boo-boos and make them better." But it sounded like she was falling back asleep and I was content to hold her.

Bryce, Arick's voice invaded my head. *Dad wants to see us again. About Navarro.*

I sighed. I needed to know how that went. Grayson had convinced Arick to let him handle the Diablo pack because he had dealt with them more than once in his days as Alpha. Given the delicacy of the situation, Arick had relented and Grayson was to meet with them yesterday.

I slid away from Ellie and pulled on sweat pants and a t-shirt and headed for the door. "Where are you off to?" Ellie asked from the bed, finally stirring.

"Arick asked me to go talk to him and his dad. I won't be long." I promised.

She slid from the bed and wrapped the dark sheet around herself. "I can't stay all day, so I'll get dressed and head back home for a bit." She stood on tiptoe to kiss me, but I stopped her. "This could be your home now." She smiled at me, absolutely radiating with joy.

"We can talk about it later. I have my shop there and need to be there in case Aunt Tessa hears from dad. I'll be back this evening or you can come stay with me." I did accept her tender kiss this time, already dreading the long day ahead without seeing her. I didn't want us to be apart again, there was a deep need in me to keep her near.

There was a brief knock at the door before it flew open and Grayson came storming in. "What the hell is this?" He asked, looking at me and then at Ellie. I frowned. "What the fuck does it look like, Uncle?"

"It looks like you're running around with the pack whore when you should be ready to help get peace back to the pack." Grayson's eyes were drilling into Ellie and I stepped between them. I was ready to punch this asshole in the face, uncle or not. "That's my mate, Uncle. You will not talk to her that way." I growled then, showing him defiance.

"The hell she is! You need to reject her. That entire family is tearing this pack apart and we could be on the brink of war with Navarro and you're up here playing footsie with a slut that started it all." Grayson was all but spitting the words out.

"What are you talking about?" Ellie asked, stepping around me as she clutched the sheet tighter.

"Navarro said you were supposed to marry one of that pack. Now you're up here with my nephew? Have you no shame at all?" Grayson looked to me and then back at Ellie.

Ellie looked at me, panic in her eyes before turning back to Grayson. "Who the hell told you that? I don't even know anyone in the Navarro pack!"

"Your father set it all up because you were whoring around with the Alpha of Cielo. Thought getting you out of that pack would be better." I couldn't believe what I was hearing and took a step back.

"You're lying. My father would never agree to that. He never told me that." Ellie turned to me then. "I swear, Bryce. I have no idea what he's talking about!"

"You're a despicable lying whore!" Grayson said and launched forward, grabbing Ellie by her throat and shoving her against the wall. I heard a wolf roar and charged forward, knocking Grayson away from Ellie as she clutched at his wrist and choked. He dropped her as I grabbed the back of his polo and pulled him away from her. "That was a mistake you won't ever make again" I promised.

Bryce. Arick's voice invaded my head as a reared back to punch his father. I released him reluctantly. "Get *out.*"

Grayson backed up then, straightening his shirt as he looked from me to Ellie and back to me. "You have two hours to get her out of this house or I'm banishing both of you." He stormed out of the room and I rushed to Ellie. She was on the floor on all fours, the sheet had fallen loose and she was gasping for breath. I shut and locked the door and pulled her close. Once she was on my lap where I sat on the floor, I looked at her neck. There was going to be a bruise and I felt rage build in my throat and vowed he would pay for touching her.

"You'll have a bruise. Are you okay?" I choked out and then looked at her face. Tears were streaming down her face. "Hey, hey, hey," I soothed. "It's okay. I've got you."

She crumpled against me, sobs racking her body. "I have no idea what he was talking about. Dad never mentioned anything about an arranged marriage, I don't know-" She mumbled some more before just sobbing against my chest and I was powerless to do anything but hold her. My mind was racing. I needed to go talk to Arick, but Ellie needed me.

Bryce. Arick called in my head.

Not now. Your dad just grabbed Ellie's throat. I answered him.

After just a moment, I heard him coming down the hallway to my door. I reached up and clicked the lock and let him in. Ellie was still sobbing and Arick knelt beside us as I held her.

"What happened?"

I shook my head, replaying everything and wasn't sure where to start.

"He said I have two hours to get rid of her or he's going to banish us both. Not that I care, but he said that Harry had set up a marriage with Navarro pack for Ellie. Did you know anything about that?" This was getting more confusing.

Arick shook his head. "No, but I don't know what was being kept from us versus what is being lied about. Nothing is making sense. Dad just took Megan to the city for safe keeping." He put his hand on Ellie's shoulder. "I'm sorry for what he did, Ellie. It doesn't matter the reason, there was no excuse for it. Mom is going to be furious."

Ellie wiped at her tears and sniffed. "Don't tell her. He's just looking out for the pack. I don't know why, but he really seems to hate our family."

Arick nodded. "Since the old days. I don't know why. Your dad has always been a great doctor and you've been like a sister to-" He stopped, seeing the mark on her shoulder. "Well, a sister to me, anyway." He glanced at me with his brows raised. I nodded, knowing he was asking if I did that. Damn right, I did.

"We need to figure out a course of action, Bryce." He said gently, which meant I had to leave Ellie here where she'd be safe.

She was already leaving me and I felt so cold without her. "I'll be fine. I have to go see Aunt Tessa anyway." She smiled at me sadly, gathered the sheet around herself and made her way to the bathroom, not meeting my eyes or Arick's. Something about her reaction had me on edge, like she didn't want me to leave and was hoping I'd choose her.

But Arick needed me, too. I raked a hand through my hair and stood. Arick clapped me on the shoulder and nodded his head to the hallway.

I followed him out, closing the door as I went. He shook his head. "You and Ellie, huh?"

"Yeah. Kind of took us both by surprise." I admitted, feeling sheepish for some reason.

Arick folded his arms across his chest and shrugged. "I thought it might be the case, but wasn't sure. You've always been so protective of her and then she left before she turned 18."

I needed to get to work so I didn't return any comments. Instead, I started with some of the questions I had. "What was Grayson on about? First he left a woman here, then he's saying all this shit with Navarro and attacking Ellie?"

Arick rubbed the back of his neck and looked down. "I don't know. None of this is making sense, but I do know that he only wants what's best for the pack. He just took Megan to the city so you and I can handle the rest. Matt is sending us some more people and another doctor. This is going to be hell."

I placed Grayson out of my mind, but this shit was going to be settled once we found out if we were going to war. "We need a plan. I don't think we're fortified enough to fire the first shot with

Diablo, but we need to be ready to return fire." Arick started down the stairs and I followed. "I agree," he said. "But how do we plan for an attack we don't know where it will be coming from?"

Matt was at the foot of the stairs as we approached and I still had the uncontrollable urge to punch him in the face. For lots of reasons, but mostly for the way he looked at Ellie last night. He clapped my shoulder as we approached and he drew a deep breath. "Congratulations, amigo on your bond. She is an incredibly amazing woman." He was smelling her on me and smiling at the thought of her on me. My hand balled into a fist, and I shrugged his hand off my shoulder. "She is." I agreed, trying to control my rage so I didn't piss off what may be our saving grace in the coming months.

Matt reached into his jacket as his cell chirped and smiled at the screen. I still wanted to punch him. "Excuse me muchachos. I must answer this." He bowed as he ducked away. "Alpha," Arick asked. "We'd like to formulate a plan with your help if you could join us in my office after that."

Matt nodded. "Of course, I will be there."

Something about his smile had me on edge.

Chapter Sixteen

Ellie

"Thank you, Matt. I appreciate your help," I said as I ran through my territory to the Diablo pack line. Matt was sitting in the passenger seat, not really saying much.

"No es problemo," he mumbled.

"Something wrong?" I asked, only playing along with his pouty man-child stance because he was helping me.

He was quiet for a moment before responding. "I am happy you will be happy, mi amor." Was all he said.

"Matt-" I began but he held up his hand.

"Spare me. It's not something you could control. I only wish the moon had been on my side this time." There was a sadness in his voice that I hadn't heard before. I sighed quietly. "There is a special woman out there for you, Matt. I know there is."

"Mi amor, I had a special woman." He smiled at me sadly and then glanced out the window. "What are you hoping comes of this meeting?"

I looked ahead at the road that stretched in front of us. "I want answers. I want to know if Grayson really met with them, and if my father arranged this marriage. Dad never said a negative word about you and I dating so I find this all a bit hard to believe."

Mat nodded. "Yes, it's very confusing. Hopefully the alpha will set the record straight."

I slowed the car down as we neared the edge of the territory. "How do we let the Alpha know we're in their territory?" I asked, actually clueless how this was done.

Matt motioned up a driveway just to the right. "We go there. The guards will let him know. And then we'll be seen."

I did as he instructed and the wrought iron gate stood foreboding in front of my car. A guard motioned for us to stop and he stepped forward.

Matt leaned over me, speaking to the guard in Spanish and the guard nodded and the gate opened. I followed the driveway around for what felt like forever.

Ellie, Bryce's voice was right behind me and I yelped.

Matt looked at me confused. "What's wrong?"

I shook my head and blocked Bryce out. "Mate link. I hadn't felt that before." I explained to Matt. I felt Bryce's anger but could no longer hear his voice and that put me on edge.

We finally arrived at the mansion, solid brick and trimmed in black with large gargoyles watching us. Guards were on the roof, heavily armed. I gulped. But there was no going back now. I had to get answers.

A guard stepped forward as we exited my car, patting us down for weapons. Once confirming there were no weapons hidden on us or around our ankles, he nodded to the guard at the door and the door was opened for us with the press of a button.

We walked into the large foyer. A grand staircase stood before us, our shoes making audible sounds on the solid marble floor. The area was extremely dark, only the light at the entrance of the stairs illuminating our path. Matt was surveying the room as best he could and I felt Bryce's panic but tried to ignore it.

"Well, well, well." Salvatore Navarro said as he began descending the stairs toward us. He was an older man, his face had seen a lot in his time. I saw his black hair was turning white but was slicked back in a vain attempt to keep that secret low. He was extremely muscular, his dark red shirt and black vest not keeping any of his body mass a secret. Tattoos wrapped around his forearm from where his sleeves were rolled up to his wrist where bracelet chains and a watch caught the dim light. He wore black slacks and shiny black shoes. This man was extremely powerful, and his icy blue gaze missed nothing as it swept me from head to toe. As he neared the bottom of the stairs, I saw his betas – both bald and extremely muscular dressed identically in black t-shirts, jeans and boots – were flanking him. We were heavily outnumbered here and I regretted not bringing my glock with me.

Matt took a step forward, "Alpha," he bowed at the waist in a show of respect.

"Shove the formalities, Matthew. We both know we don't like each other." He motioned to a door to his left, our right. "Shall we have a drink and we can discuss what it is you think you want from me?" He didn't wait for an answer. Instead he led us to what turned out to be a large study with bookshelf lined walls and a fireplace with a small fire in it. Sofas sat facing each other in front of the fire and he took a seat on one and motioned for us to do the same on the opposite one while his beta poured drinks.

I smelled the scotch, similar to what my father drank and politely nipped at it, not wanting my senses dulled. Matt and Sal saluted each other and threw it back easily. Sal handed his glass back to his beta for another, but Matt declined.

"I won't waste time, Alpha. I'm sure you're extremely busy." Matt began. "I want to know what business you have with Dr. Savoy."

Sal's eyes lowered for a moment. "That name keeps coming up lately. Honestly, I have no idea how I got thrown into this, but I'm tired of it." He looked at me then. "Can you explain to me why your pack seems to think I know anything about it?"

I swallowed and sat my glass down. "I'll be completely honest with you, I don't know anything other than my father's truck was found near our borders. He wasn't with it but his pain meds were missing."

Matt watched Sal carefully. "There's more. One of my rogues broke into her home looking for something, amigo. They said someone from your pack hired him."

Sal kind of chuckled and rubbed his chin as he leaned forward on his knees. "That could be, I don't keep close watch on what my pack does outside of our territory." He looked at his betas, now standing by the door. "Until it crosses paths with another pack."

"I understand the previous Alpha came to see you." Matt offered this, his eyes narrowed on Sal in suspicion. Sal shook his head. "I haven't heard from him since he turned the pack over to Arick.

And good riddance. He tried to sell his pack out to my uncle before I took the pack."

"I don't understand," I said – extremely confused.

"There is a chunk of land to the west of your territory that is incredibly valuable to the Ciello pack because of where it's located. It's right in the middle of the two territories and off the main drag to the city to the north. Very valuable deal." Sal cocked his head to the side. "Many years ago, Grayson started trying to build houses there on his own with no capital. He came to me for my help. I told him there was nothing I could do because I didn't have the pack. A week later, my uncle died suddenly." He looked from me to Matt and back again. "I took the pack and provided the cash to Grayson. But everything fell through. He owed me a lot of money."

My mind was racing trying to keep up. Grayson not only owed a lot of money to the Diablo pack, but he had lied about coming to see the Alpha, too? "Has he paid any of that back?"

Sal leaned back and draped his arms across the back of the sofa. "He has made some small payments. But then I said enough was enough and I wanted the land myself. I could broker a deal that would make my money almost double now that production in the city is going up and people are moving in. But he said he had to take care of a few things first. Your brother was very much against Grayson doing business with me." He looked at me and his eyes drilled into me.

"So you arranged for her to marry someone in your pack?"

"No, Grayson offered to sell her to my pack because she was turning rogue. I turned him down, I have no interest in buying my women. Perhaps I should have reconsidered." His gaze moved over me slowly and I fought the urge to squirm. "You don't look very rogue to me. Are you a wildling in bed, senorita?"

Matt stood then. "I think we have enough for now. I won't waste anymore of your time."

He started toward the door and the betas stood in the way. I stood, watching the situation almost in slow motion. "You came to the heart of the pack and got my information. What are you going to give to me, Matthew?"

Matt turned slowly. "What is it that you want?"

Sal eyed me before answering. "I want the Shadow wolf pack. Grayson has done nothing but given me a bunch of lies. I have no money to show for it, I want what is owed to me." He swung his gaze back to Matt. "With interest."

Matt swept his arms wide. "I have no quarrel with you or the Shadow pack. That should be with you and Alpha Arick to figure out."

"Arick is refusing to talk to me. His father is the only one that calls on my attention. It's rude as an Alpha, if I am being completely honest." He looked bored as he studied his fingernails. "I want you to arrange it, Matthew. As a favor from your father to my uncle. They were dear friends, if you'll remember."

I took a deep breath. "I will talk to Alpha Arick myself. I am sure there has been a misunderstanding."

"Oh my sweet. According to Grayson you have no pull with that pack any longer. He ran you off, didn't he?" My chin came up at his condensation.

"She is mated with Arick's beta. She can talk through him." Matt acknowledged, trying to calm the situation down.

"My, my. This is a pleasant surprise." Sal said as he stood now, coming to stand in front of me. "I think we now have what we need to proceed to get what I want." He motioned to Matt. "Go back to that Alpha. Let him know we have the Beta's mate and I want to bargain." Sal turned to Matt and motioned with his chin. "My beta will see to it you're returned to the Shadow Wolf pack to give them my message. But this sweetness," he said as he cupped my chin. "Will stay here with me until I hear from Arick."

"You can't-" Matt began and Sal turned into full fury the next moment, booming in his alpha voice. "I am the Alpha! I can do as I please. Now, leave." He motioned with his hand, his gaze coming back to me. I saw something in his eyes that didn't sit well with me and I began to shake.

"Don't fret, my sweet. Nothing will happen to you as long as your alpha co-operates." The Beta took Matt's arm and pulled him from the room, Matt unable to argue with Sal any longer.

He turned and walked to his desk and picked up the phone. "We have a guest I need taken care of." And he replaced the receiver. In the next moment, three guards came into the room, armed and in full tactical gear. "Gosh," I said. "You sent an army for little ol' me?"

Sal laughed then. "I heard what you did to that Cielo mongrel. I won't take a chance." He then nodded in my direction and the guards grabbed my arms and pulled me from the room. I was led up the large staircase and around to the right before a dark mahogany door was unlocked and I was shoved into a bedroom. It was dark, but once I was alone, I listened to the lock click and then walked to the window. I threw the heavy drapes back and gray light came into the room. I could see the front of the house, my car still in the driveway below. I heard the guards outside the door talking and sighed. It was going to be a long day. I laid down on the bed and thought through my options.

I finally just closed my eyes and pictured Bryce. I tried to reach him through our new link, but there was nothing returned and realized our link wasn't strong while I was off our territory.

Okay, that was a bust. The windows were sealed and nailed shut. So I could break the glass, but then they'd likely hear me and I was screwed. I was fairly certain they wouldn't kill me, but hurting me wasn't off the table.

I began pacing, knowing that it was only a matter of time until I got a chance to do something and I'd have to stay sharp to jump on it when it happened. I wasn't sure how much time had passed, but the light outside was starting to dim. Still no rain yet, but maybe we'd get lucky.

The guards outside the door fell silent and I peeked out the window again. My car was still there, that likely meant the key was still there, too. I drummed my fingers on the window sill, not enjoying my current situation at all. Then I heard something and I peered up the driveway. A familiar black Yamaha was creeping slowly up the driveway and I heard the throttle rev when the rider saw my white car. This was it, this was going to happen.

I began searching the room. Something heavy. As the moon would have it, I located a led crystal ashtray. It should do the trick. Saying a silent "sorry," I stood behind the door and threw the ashtray against the window as loud as I could and screamed.

I heard a key jingle and knew the guard was coming in. Once he swung the door open, I kicked it back on it and it caused him to jar and he dropped the gun. I picked it up and hit him across the face and he fell to the ground with the thump. I didn't think I'd knock him out, but I was glad what Matt had taught me wasn't completely lost. Once outside the door, I looked down the hallways to make sure no one saw me and started down the stairs to the front door. I heard fighting on the other side of the door and knew Bryce was trying to fight his way in. I raised the gun and fired off several rounds to get everyone to duck and then charged to the front door. "Bryce! Gotta go!" I screamed as I ran past him and jumped into my car.

He was in the passenger seat in a heartbeat, ripping his helmet off as I spun tires on the pavement and raced down the driveway. I heard shouting behind us but didn't glance back as I sped even faster. "Fence, Ellie. Fence!" Bryce yelled and braced himself for a front end impact.

"Relax," I said as I continued my speed and then shifted to neutral, whipped the wheel and slid sideways into the gate, ripping it off its hinges. We tail spinned for several spins, taking out several plants and I saw the guard dive out of the way of my car. We reached the road quickly and I shifted into gear and took off toward our territory. I heard engines rev behind us and only now did I glance back. Bryce also looked behind us and exclaimed. "Fuck!" Just before he grabbed my neck and pushed my head down. The back window splintered as bullets started flying into my car.

I reached down by my right knee and pulled loose the gun I had stored there and handed it to Bryce. "Keep your head down!" He said before he saw the gun in my hand and took it from me.

He aimed behind us but couldn't see through the glass. "Shit, the glass is all fucked up. I can't see."

Keeping my eyes on the road and my foot firmly on the accelerator, I dropped another gear to put some distance between us and the vehicle swung in behind us. "Get ready." I said and reached across Bryce's lap.

"For what?" He asked before he was thrown back into the backseat of the car when I released the back of his seat.

"Sorry," I said. "Kick the back window out." He could now move around in the cabin of the car easily, despite his size. Which is how I had modified the car. I heard him knock the back glass out and begin firing at the SUV behind us. I moved around on the road enough that their bullets weren't going to hit us, but that meant that he couldn't get a shot, either. There was a motorcycle closing on us and I knew I couldn't outrun it, so I slowed until it could catch up to us. I reached across to the glove compartment and pulled out my backup gun and lowered my window. My hair was whipping around my face and adrenaline was making my heart race.

Then I shot his front tire out.

From the mirror, I could see it flip and the driver went flying into the high grass on the side of the road. The bike was dealt with, but the SUV wasn't letting us out of sight. "Bryce, passenger side. Get ready."

I lowered his window and dropped speed until we were side by side with the SUV. He crawled forward until he was clear of the window and shot the back tire and it began to wobble on the road. I dropped gear again and sped in front of the SUV and in my rear view mirror I saw it flip onto its side and slide several feet.

Bryce's breathing was heavy and labored and all he could mutter was "holy shit, holy shit."

I remembered reacting very similarly to my first high speed chase with Matt, too. But I had won that round, too.

I heard him click the safety on the gun and put it in the glove compartment and I did the same with mine, watching the road. It was starting to rain now.

"We're in our territory now. Pull over somewhere." Bryce told me sternly.

"Are you hurt?" I asked, concerned.

"Just do it, Ellie." He sounded furious so I found a small field we wouldn't be seen easily in the rain and pulled in. Then I realized my right headlight wasn't working because of the gate and I got sad. My poor car.

He rolled the windows up to keep the rain out and pulled the seat back up.

He put his hands out in front of him on the dash and kind of turned to me. "What was-" he started, then stopped. "How do you-" he stopped again and then ran his hands through his hair. "How the fuck did you know to do that?" He was flabbergasted, which I guess I had expected. My adrenaline was crashing and I was getting sleepy suddenly.

I shrugged, not ready to deal with this right now. Grayson had done the pack dirty and he was worried how I knew how to avoid the mob? "Don't shrug me off. What have you been doing for 10 years?" He asked.

I sighed. "Mostly chop shop jobs, a few custom jobs on cars. Not all of it was legitimate. And we got into some bad situations." That was the light version of it. I had been slapped across the face with a pistol, I had evaded police, but this was the first time I'd had to explain it.

"Who is we?" He asked, raising one eyebrow.

I threw my head against my seat, sighed and closed my eyes. "Matt and I. We were both on the wrong side of the law more than . . . well, more than a handful of times."

I heard him scrub at his face, not sure what he was feeling. A small part of me wondered if he was going to send me away now that he knew the truth. I watched the rain fall down the windows and tried not to think about the pain suddenly exploding in my chest at the thought.

"I'm going to murder that son of a bitch." He finally said quietly, staring straight ahead at the field we were sitting in.

"It wasn't Matt's fault. After Tanner died, I didn't care if I died or not. Matt had nothing to do with my choices. They were mine to make.." My vision blurred as my voice raised through my rant. He looked at me then and I felt tears clog my throat. It had to be the adrenaline crash, but I was suddenly stifled in the air of the car and I didn't care if it was raining I had to get out of there. I opened my door, fighting the tall grass with my door and then I was out and took off running in the field. I started to shift into my wolf but then there was an arm on my shoulder, stopping me and turning me around. I faced him, tears mingling with the rain.

Bryce cupped my face. "You are so fucking amazing, Ellie. I'm so scared and turned on at the same time. I am upset, but because I thought I was going to lose you right after I found you again. I can't imagine a world you're not in it with me. And I was terrified when I saw Matt coming back without you. I don't know what possessed

~ 221 ~

you to do something so fucking bone headed and put yourself in danger and I just couldn't stop but thinking what I would do if-"

He didn't finish the thought but instead mashed his lips to mine, kissing my bottom lip and then my top lip before shoving into my mouth with his tongue. He held my head in place so I couldn't escape and I didn't want to. I started grabbing at his clothes, wanting to feel his skin on mine in a primal way only mates could experience. I took everything off of him and fell to my back with him on me while he was still kissing me. The wet grass was cool on my skin as he shoved my jeans down my legs and I kicked them off, needing to feel him deep within me. He thumbed my breasts through my shirt and in the next minute he was frantically thrusting into me, filling me with a white hot heat at my very core. He kissed down my neck and began nipping me, leaving a mark. Marking me as his. "Oh my fucking God, Ellie. I love you so much." He said as he braced his forehead against mine, slowing his strokes and catching his breath. "Don't ever leave me again. Please. I couldn't live without you." And then he was kissing me again, stealing my breath and any thought of a response I could have given him.

We both exploded at the same time, my screams lost in the rain as I convulsed around him. He held me close to his chest, planting little kisses on me as the rain pelted my skin, cooling me while the passion we had just shared still raced through me and warmed me.

He smoothed my hair away from my face, which was a vain attempt because it was so matted from the wind, rain and well, sex. "Promise me." He asked of me, searching my eyes.

"Promise what?" I asked, but I knew what he was going to ask. It was written all over his face.

"Promise me that you'll talk to me before you do something like that again. Baby, please. I don't think you understand how much I care about you." He kissed me gently to punctuate his declaration. "I hope that one day you'll love me half as much as I love you. I was a complete and total jackass to ever let you leave a decade ago. And I won't be without you ever again. Promise me."

My heart was racing at his words. I didn't know how long I had waited for him to care about me, to return my affection and it felt like a bomb going off in my chest of sheer joy. I smiled at him. "Well," I said coyly. "To be fair, if you had been attracted to a 14 year old it would have been a little creepy." I laughed.

"Ellie." He said as a dark warning.

I sobered a bit, and then met his eyes. "I have loved you since I was a young girl. You were all I ever wanted. I promise you won't be without me." The smile that lit his face was worth everything in this world. It was pure happiness and I had never seen it on him before. He gently kissed me then and I realized the rain had stopped and we were in the middle of a field somewhere on our main highway, he was naked and I was all but naked. I looked around and he stood then, offering me his hand. I took it and he pulled me to my feet, even though my knees were a little weak.

I sought out my jeans, but they were wet and impossible to put on. I did pull my panties on so there was at least that and I caught him staring at me, this dazed look on his face. "What's wrong?" I asked.

He didn't answer me, just walked over to where I stood. The ground made squishy noises as his steps gentled and he placed a hand on my cold, wet, exposed belly.

"What is it?" I asked him, genuinely concerned.

"We couldn't have pups before, we weren't mated. But you could be pregnant now. You could have my baby deep inside you right now." I froze in my tracks.

Was I ready for something like that? Could I even begin to be ready for something like that with all this shit going on between the packs? We were on the brink of war, I had been kidnapped today and we still had little to no answers. And then, is that happiness that he's feeling? Regret? Worry?

He cupped my cheek and pulled me close. "I'd love for you to be the mother of my children if the moon wants that. You'd be an excellent mother, you're an amazing woman. I would be so lucky."

I shivered in his arms, not sure how I felt about any of this.

"We need to find my dad first," I said and my teeth started chattering. He pulled me close and lifted me into his arms. My legs went around him and my arms circled his neck as he carried me back to the car. All I could do was shake and shiver, scared and feeling desperate to get back on my own timeline and not someone else's.

"Shhh, it's okay." He soothed in my hair as we walked, like carrying me with one arm was nothing. I didn't say anything, I was trembling too wildly. He wore only his jeans as we neared my car. I hadn't realized we'd run so far away, but he seemed to know exactly where to find it.

He put me in the passenger seat and the warmth of the car helped a little. In no time, he had my car back on the road, even though she was making some noises I knew I'd have to fix later. I was worried to look at the damage. I had taken out a gate and a bunch of shrubbery. It wasn't going to be pretty.

Arick was waiting for us when we got there. Bryce must have called out to him. The maid brought Bryce a blanket that he wrapped around me and carried me to the study where he sat me down on the couch and rubbed my arms. Arick started a fire and no one said anything as they stared at me. Something hot to drink was put in my hands and I sipped at it, staring at the fire in front of me.

"Well," Arick said finally, running a hand over the top of his long hair. He hadn't bothered to tie it up and it fell to his shoulders and was slightly matted. Like he had slept that way. "Did you learn anything?"

I looked at him then. "Matt didn't bring you up to speed?"

"Only some of it. I'd like to know how you got out of there and what you found out about your father." I narrowed my eyes at him as he spoke.

"Grayson put the pack in deep shit, that's what happened." I said, now really pissed off. "But Salvatore didn't seem to know anything about my father's dealings with the Diablo pack."

Arick squatted down in front of me and looked at me. "This is me, Ellie. We've known each other a long time. You can tell me."

I took a deep breath. Hot chocolate was what I had been handed. It smelled good and was warming me from the inside out. "That plot of land that the construction was started on and never finished belongs to the pack. Grayson had taken out a large loan from the Diablo pack to do construction but it all fell through. And now

Grayson owes a ton of money to the Diablo pack. And they want it paid back with interest."

Arick and Bryce looked at each other. "What about your arranged marriage through your father?" Arick asked now, his eyes not leaving Bryce.

I shook my head and stared back into the fire. "Salvatore said Grayson offered me up to align our packs and to keep me from going rogue. He said he should have reconsidered." A shudder moved through me and I felt Bryce's arm around my shoulders then. "But he also said Grayson hadn't been to the pack to talk to him like he had told us. Sal said he hadn't seen him in awhile. Since he defaulted on the loan. Now Sal wants the land and interest on the loan." I heaved a breath, happy that part was over with. If what Salvatore had said was true, Grayson had sold out his own pack, which was punishable by death.

"I want to go home," I mumbled before sipping the hot drink again.

"Where is Grayson now?" Bryce asked. Arick heaved a deep sigh and stood. "He took Megan to the city to be safe. We need to go get her."

Arick was already moving to the door. Bryce was obviously torn where to go. I saw it on his face. "Go get Megan. Keep her safe." I smiled weakly. "I'll be here when you get back." He kissed me for a long moment before standing to leave. "I will be back. I love you, Ellie."

I yawned and stretched. "I love you, Bryce. Hurry back." I leaned against the pillows and my eyes closed, crashing from the adrenaline. Sleep finally took me under.

I don't know how long I slept before waking to pain exploding across the left half of my face. I felt myself falling to the floor and I hit something as I fell because the wind rushed out of my lungs.

I opened my eyes, blinking rapidly. In the dim room I realized I wasn't alone. A figure stood over me. "You really are a stubborn little slut, aren't you?" I recognized Grayson's voice. I quickly surmised that he had hit me across the face with something in his hand and blood was pooling inside my jaw. He had kicked me in my stomach and I was still struggling to get air in my lungs. "All you had to do was just go away, go back to the city and nothing had to happen to anyone else."

He reared back to kick me again and I rolled out of the way and took his ankles out from under him and he fell with a crash to the table, his head cracking on the hard edge. He held his head for a moment as I scrambled to my feet. "You bitch!" He spat as he stood again. He now pointed his gun at me and I froze, assessing the situation around the pain in my head and the tingling I felt in my face, telling me that it was swelling. I was having trouble keeping that eye open. The only light in the room came from the lamp on Arick's desk and that was behind Grayson, which meant he could see me better than I could see him. Time to use the noggin, Ellie.

"So you were behind all of it? Did you kill Tanner, too? Like you did with Alyssa?" I had to get him talking, men like him got sloppy when they were talking.

"I didn't cut the cable myself. But wolves are very easily influenced by jealousy. All I had to do was let it slip that Tanner was sleeping with someone's mate and they took care of it for me." Rage boiled up inside me at his casual admission. Like it wasn't a life, like it wasn't my brother and his son's best friend that had been stolen.

"Alyssa saw other Diablo pack wolves over at the property and got nosy. She had to be dealt with. Then your father went and got that piece of shit motorcycle and I knew it was only a matter of time before one of you saw the break line. I tried to stop it, but he just wouldn't listen to me."

I swallowed, my blood running cold. "Did you kill him, too?"

"No, he's someplace for safe keeping. I had planned to use him to get you under control. But then Bryce just wouldn't leave you alone and I couldn't get an opportunity to play that card." His voice was so casual, like he was talking about things he had wanted to do this weekend instead of dabbling in other people's lives.

"My nephew is going to come back to find you dead in a field somewhere and assume that Sal had something to do with it and then I'll have your father disposed of."

"None of this makes sense. Why did it all start with Tanner? What did he ever do to you?" Tears were falling from my good eye. I couldn't tell if the other one was or not because of the swelling.

"He got nosey, wondering why I was talking to Sal so much. They were another pack, weren't they? What could they have that we need? He just wouldn't let it go. And then he was snooping and heard a call I was on. I had promised Sal a lot of interest on that loan. If Tanner had told Arick anything it could have been all over."

So Tanner had stumbled into a truth he probably hadn't even known he had. "This will all come to light, you know. We went to see Sal today."

Grayson scoffed and stood straighter. "I doubt Arick will believe anything you've said once you write the note you're running off for something better." He cocked the gun back and nodded toward the door. "Move." I didn't move at first and he took two steps closer and I felt the gun in my arm. "I said, move, bitch."

I saw my chance and threw my weight toward him, knocking the gun farther to his right so the shot that fired hit a bookcase and then we were on the ground, fighting for control of the gun. My knee connected with something and he grunted, but he was a lot bigger than I was and it didn't really phase me at all as we continued to roll around on the study floor. "You fucking whore!" He screamed and another shot squeezed off. The recoil unsettled him enough I saw my chance and arched my back and connected my head to his sternum. He grunted and dragged in a breath then and I wrapped my legs around his and flipped him until I was on top of him and I was able to wedge my knee against his throat. His right arm swung toward me and I braced for it, but instead a tattooed hand grabbed his wrist as I was lifted off his chest by stronger arms. I was still angry and began fighting against whoever had pulled me off of him.

"Let me go!" I screamed. "He murdered my brother! I'm going to fucking *kill* him."

I was scratching and clawing at anything I could get, blinded by the rage I felt burning in me. Whoever was holding me pulled me toward the study door and finally, Bryce came into my peripheral vision and I stopped long enough to look at him. His mouth dropped open as he saw my bruised and swollen face. I had to look awful.

In the next instant, he was on Grayson, knocking him down and pummeling his face as he knelt over Grayson's chest. "Did you feel like a man doing that to a woman's face, Uncle?" He was spitting the words he was so mad and I didn't know what to do. Arick stepped forward and put a hand on Bryce's shoulder. Using his Alpha voice, he breathed "stop" and Bryce's arms stopped immediately. Grayson was on the floor, breathing but not really recognizable. His eyes were swollen shut, his lip was split and there was blood all over his teeth.

Arick picked Grayson up now, forcing Bryce to step back. I moved forward, but Bryce stood between my vision and Grayson. I was kind of relieved. Carrying Grayson by his collar to the front of the house, his eyes cold with fury, the door swung open to meet them. Sal stood there now, a smile curving his lips.

"Grayson," he said now. "You don't call, you don't write. I started to think you didn't want to see me. And we both know how much I wanted to see you."

Sal turned to the men standing behind him and nodded. They moved forward and gathered Grayson from Arick and took him down the front of the stairs and threw him in the back of an all black SUV and sped away. Sal then turned to where I stood behind Bryce and did a sweeping bow. "My lady, I do apologize for this afternoon. I heard how well you took care of my men. If you ever decide to rethink Grayson's offer and come to the Diablo pack, please let us know. In the meantime, I discovered something that you may wish returned to you."

He nodded to the SUV waiting at the bottom of the steps and the back door opened and Dad stumbled out of it, dazed and looking around. "Daddy!" I screamed as I ran past Bryce to him. His face was covered in yellowing bruises.. Blood crusted his lip still, but he seemed okay.

"Oh baby, oh my Ellie." He held me and I could only sob as I felt his warm embrace. He was clutching the back of my head to his shoulder. "I thought I had lost you." He said now.

Sal bowed one more time to Arick and came down the steps, climbed into the passenger seat of the SUV and like they were never here, they faded into the night. I turned toward the house and looked from Bryce to Arick. His eyes were like steel, revealing nothing. I only looked at him. "He betrayed this pack and tried to sell us out to the highest bidder. He is dead to me." And with that finality, he spoke the last words over his father's life with the pack. I was conflicted, knowing my brother's death had been avenged with him being banished but I knew that meant Arick had just lost his father.

"I'm sorry, Arick." The look that he gave me made my blood almost stop. I had never seen a dark side to Arick, but it was there now. "He made his choices." I swallowed nervously and nodded. Dad grunted beside me. "Let me get you home, Dad."

"It is late," Arick said. "I must insist your father make use of one of the guest rooms and we can discuss in the morning what else has to be done." I was sure Arick meant he still had questions he wanted answers to before it got through the pack what had happened here tonight. I nodded at Dad, who was looking at me.

"Thank you, Alpha." Dad said and made the long walk up the steps to the house. Bryce was looking at me as I helped him up the steps, his legs weren't sturdy. "So you and Bryce are finally mated?" Dad asked now. Bryce's face split in a grin. "Yes, sir."

Dad clapped him on the shoulder as we walked by. "Welcome to the family, son. Again."

Together, Bryce and I got dad comfortable in one of the guest rooms. I stayed behind getting him in the shower and into bed to make sure he was okay. Arick had food sent up and I got that in place for him before slipping from the room, relieved he was okay and alive. I had my dad back. As I closed the door and turned, I crashed into Megan.

She was standing in the dark hallway with tears in her eyes. "I heard what happened. Are you okay? You look awful."

I kind of laughed. "I'm okay now. Dad is home and safe." I wanted to add that I knew what happened to my brother, but then I didn't because Megan didn't know that Grayson had anything to do with that. "I heard Dad banished Grandpa." Megan said with a shaky voice.

"Yes, he did." Was all I said. I wasn't sure how to help Megan handle this. But I did think to add "loyalty is all we have as a family. And it means everything."

Megan nodded before hugging me and I winced. My ribs still hurt from earlier. "I'm so sorry Grandpa did that to you, Ellie. Please don't think we're all like that."

I soothed her hair and held her tight against me. "I don't think that at all. I know you're not like that. I know your dad isn't like that." I kissed the top of her head. "Come on, I'll get you into bed and then I need to dress these wounds."

"I'm okay," she said, stepping back and wiping her tears. "I just wanted to know you're okay."

She went down the hallway to her room and I watched her until she was in her room. I sighed with relief and went to Bryce's-our- room. I hadn't really thought about where we would live, but with Bryce being the Beta it would make sense for it to be here. My garage would stay at Dad's house so strangers weren't on Alpha grounds.

When I entered the room, Bryce was sitting at the foot of his bed, holding his head in his hands. I looked around the room and then back at Bryce after seeing nothing amiss. "What's wrong?"

He looked up at me then and relief flooded his features. "I'm really glad you're okay, is all."

I smiled. "Yes, I'm okay. Just sore." Then I straightened and frowned. "How did you time it so well to walk in on Grayson and I fighting?"

"Well," He said and put his hands in his pocket. "Matt came back from Diablo earlier without you and we sent him to the city to get Grayson since it's closer to his pack and he could put his foot down and make Grayson come back here. When he got to the penthouse, Megan was alone and Grayson was already gone. So Matt called us and we went and got Sal." He paused and rubbed the back of his neck. "So Arick and Sal cleared the air and went through it. We figured out that Tanner must have found something out about Grayson and the development of that land and-" he stopped and released a breath. "Well, anyway. Sal was more than happy to take the payment of the loan so that our packs were square. But then when asked what would happen here, Arick told Sal he would be banished. So Sal wanted a piece of him, first."

I sat down on the bed and laid back after a minute. "I feel so terrible for Arick. That can't be easy to deal with and he was just so cold. I've never seen him like that before." Bryce sat down next to me, leaning over my body. He took my left hand in his and ran his thumb on the diamond still there. "Don't ever scare the shit out of me like that again, Ellie. These last 24 hours have taken years off the end of my life."

I laughed at him then. "I didn't have a choice and I certainly didn't want my face punched in or to be shot at."

"Yeah, about that. We need to talk about that car, James Bond."

I sat up. "What do you mean?" He couldn't mean I was going to have to get rid of my car.

"Well, I don't see the need for you to have a gun in the glove box and one strapped to under the steering wheel. You also likely won't need the seat to go all the way back, either." He stopped and narrowed his eyes. "Wait, I have to think about that one a bit more."

I laughed and shoved him off of me and went to the shower. My face was now fully swollen and it hurt to talk or smile. "I'm not getting rid of anything in that car. I did it all myself right up to printing the holsters."

I heard him heave a sigh as I took clothes off. My ribs were bruising and I grimaced as I touched them while looking in the mirror. Bryce now stood behind me, his expression dark. "Grayson had better hope I never get a chance to go at him again." He touched my shoulders carefully and kissed the side of my neck. I leaned against his warmth reveled in the feeling of belonging to him.

"We'll need to meet with Arick tomorrow and Dad and figure out what our next move is. Do you know if Matt is still here?" I asked him now. I didn't miss how Bryce tensed behind me at the mention of the other Alpha. "Oh yeah, he's sniffing around somewhere."

I turned and stepped into his waiting arms and held him tight. "Matt didn't want to go with me to Sal's. But I told him that if he didn't go with me, I would have to go by myself and then he gave in."

"Well, that doesn't make me like him anymore. He should have told me." I chuckled against his chest, soaking in his warmth. "He knew that I'd just take off while he did that. So he did what he thought was best." I pulled away from him and raised my right hand. "Scout's honor, he did nothing to me while we were gone."

He smiled slightly and then sobered almost right away. "Did Sal's guys do anything? To you, I mean?"

I shook my head and grimaced. "No, but I probably owe one some flowers for knocking him out cold." Bryce laughed and pulled me close. "That's my girl. I don't know why I ever thought you couldn't handle yourself." He rolled his eyes. "You're so incredible, Ellie."

We held each other for a moment longer, neither one of us wanting to be away from the other, but I yawned and broke the moment. Bryce carefully showered me, washing all my bumps and scrapes and I washed his knuckles and kissed the pain away.

We settled into his bed after, content to be with each other and drifted off to a deep sleep, knowing we were where we belonged.

Chapter Seventeen

Ellie

The next day, it was almost noon before I stirred. Bryce was already gone, which I was almost grateful for because my face had to look as horrific as it felt. My ribs were bruised and it hurt to breathe, so I was going to have to take it easy. Dad might have an idea. That brought me straight up in bed. Dad was home. I could see him, talk to him and hug him.

I dressed quickly, desperately needing coffee. I saw it was just after 10 in the morning so it wasn't terrible, all things considered. But I had wanted to talk to the guys in my life all together. Because if I knew anything about them, plans were being made that I wasn't a part of.

I went to Arick's study and dad was there with Arick. No Bryce. Dad stood and hugged me when I walked in and then we both sat across from Arick. Where was Bryce? "Your dad and I were catching up the last couple of weeks. Da-" he stopped and cleared his throat. "Grayson had been worried that your dad would find the severed brake line on Tanner's bike. So he had taken him and held him until he could figure out damage control. Then when Sal had said no to Grayson's proposal to marry you off, Grayson was going to get rid of you, too, Ellie."

He lowered his eyes. "I'm sorry I didn't keep you safe. Both of you." He looked back at us before either one of us could speak. "But the pack owes you both everything. Ellie, if you hadn't been so strong we wouldn't have aligned our pack with Cielo and Diablo. So, thank you. Both of you."

I nodded. I hadn't done anything other than survive. Dad had been through it a lot harder, judging by the swelling and bruising on his face. I met Arick's gaze. "What about the wolf that cut Tanner's brake line? Do we know who he is?"

Arick shook his head. "No, sadly. It had to be someone who was here that night because Tanner had brought the bike here and then we had left from here to ride. But it's been ten years and staffing has changed. I'm sure that wolf is long gone by now."

I didn't like that answer, but I would live with it, at least. Ultimately, the person that was responsible for it had been dealt with. Matt entered the study then and placed a hand on my shoulder. "I'm glad you're home safe," he said to me and his voice was quiet, intimate. I laid my hand over his and patted it. "Me, too. Thanks for sending the calvary in to get me."

Matt laughed and sat down on the soft. "From what I heard, he was just a distraction while you did the heavy lifting." He shook his head and rubbed his eyes. "Bryce is incredibly lucky to have you, Ellie." I noticed Dad looking from Matt to me and back again. "Dad," I said now. "This is Matt. He's the Alpha of Cielo." They shook hands and Dad looked him up and down. "And very familiar with my daughter, I see." Matt nodded. "Proudly, sir. She's an awesome woman."

"Yes, she is." Bryce's voice sounded from the doorway.

I turned and smiled at him, so happy to see him. Warmth bloomed through me as he came into the room and all I could feel was him.

"I must be getting back to the city," Matt said now and shook Arick's hand. "Let me know what you decide, Alpha." Arick nodded. As Matt walked by, he cast one more glance at me, sadness evident in his eyes. He clapped Bryce on the shoulder and smiled sadly as he walked away.

"Decide?" I asked Arick after Matt was gone.

"About the project land at the edge of town." Arick said, sitting back down behind his desk. "Alpha wants in on the deal and knows of a firm that could begin designs."

I nodded and looked at my dad. "We should get you home so we can send Tessa and Wade home, Dad."

Arick sent for a car to take us home, and I frowned at him. "I can just drive my car." He shook his head with a wince. "She leaked fluid all over the place. We can have her towed later."

I wanted to cry. My baby.

Bryce put his arms around me and we went outside and got Dad into the SUV and were on our way to my house. Everyone in the car was quiet and I noticed Dad looking at me suspiciously. "What?" I asked.

He shook his head and looked out the window. "Nothing. Did you two decide where you're going to live?" I looked at Bryce then. We hadn't really talked about it. Bryce was the Beta and needed to be at the pack house, but I was the pack mechanic and needed my garage. "We haven't thought it through, no. Everything kind of happened really fast," I answered finally.

"We can let things settle down for a while before we make a big deal." Bryce said, holding my eyes. But his eyes showed sadness. "In the meantime, with your permission, sir." He turned to dad. "I'd like to stay with Ellie while she gets you settled."

Dad smiled then and nodded. "Of course. It'll be good to get settled in knowing I have a live-in protector." He chuckled as the SUV pulled to a stop in front of the house. Tessa came out front and cried out when Dad stepped out of the car and smiled at her. "Hey, Tessa. Long time no see." She threw her arms around her brother in-law and tears were in her eyes. "I thought we'd lost you, Harry."

He laughed as he stepped out of her embrace. "Yeah, I thought I was a goner a few times, too."

"What happened?" She asked, her brow furrowed in concern.

"Long story," he said. "I just want to be home."

Tessa started chatting about what Wade had been working on while Harry had been gone. The rest of the day was in a blur as Wade caught dad up on everything he had missed and we talked and had dinner as a family, which was a welcome change and I felt a sense of warmth and belonging I hadn't felt in a decade. This was my family, it was complete for the first time since I lost Tanner.

I smiled sadly, wishing he could see this. Could be a part of this.

He is always with us, mate. Bryce said in my mind.

I looked at him, his eyes on me. I loved how he was in and around my mind, a part of me. I held his hand under the table and smiled at him.

That night as he held me in the moonlight in my room, my ribs still too sore to do anything physically, he stroked my shoulder with one hand and we listened to each other's heartbeat.

"Well," he said now. "What are we going to do about where we live?"

I had been dreading this conversation. Because my day-job was here at Dad's and he wanted me to be a Beta's wife and help fill in since there was no Luna. "I hadn't really thought a lot about it," I said, propping myself up to look at him. "I want to come here daily to work on cars. But I can live at the pack house if you want me, too."

He stroked my cheek with his index finger before cupping my face. "You don't have to work if you don't want to. We can find another pack mechanic."

"But I want to do it. This is why I'm here and I love working on them."

He nodded, hearing the sternness in my voice. "We can talk through it when things settle down," he said again. Which meant we were not done talking about it. He didn't want me to do anything other than be a beta wife? No, thank you.

"Stop thinking," he softly said and kissed me tenderly, rolling me to my back. "I just want you to be happy," he said as he nuzzled closer to my neck. "Okay," I said. "We'll talk it through." But then all my thoughts were stolen from me as he kissed his way down my abdomen, making it clear while I was too sore to do anything, he wasn't.

So he spent the rest of the night worshiping me with his lips.

~*~

When I woke up the next morning, he was already gone. I frowned at the bed and looked around the room. I was greeted with silence as I moved from the bed, looking for him.

Where did you go? I asked him.

I had something to take care of. I'll be there soon, love. He responded and I relaxed. I dressed and went down in search of coffee. My dad and Tessa were already in the kitchen and food was being cooked. I wasn't hungry, but it did smell good. In the next few moments Wade floated in and began inhaling pancakes, bacon and toast like he hadn't eaten in a month.

"Are you still going to be the mechanic for the pack?" Dad asked now from his chair at the kitchen table.

"That's my plan, yes. You built that garage for me. And in the two weeks I've been home I haven't had a single customer." Not that I'd had time, I reminded myself. Between Bryce suddenly being the center of my day and having to hunt down dad, nothing would have gotten done.

Harry nodded and turned to Tessa. "How long are you and Wade staying in town?"

Tessa flipped her spatula around and shrugged. "As long as you need Wade's help. I know it's a lot with the pups coming."

Tessa turned to me and looked me from head to toe. "Did you tell her yet?" She asked my dad now.

"Tell me what?" My eyes switched between the two quickly.

Harry shook his head. "Nothing. We'll talk about it later."

I sighed and sat my coffee aside. "You pig-headed men. If one more man tells me 'we'll talk later' I'm going to scream the house down."

Harry opened his mouth to rebuttal but we heard an army of trucks pulling up beside the house. I frowned at everyone and they all shrugged at me. I went down the steps to the basement and opened the garage doors. Three tow trucks with their caution flashers on were sitting outside my garage. Each one had at least one vehicle behind it, the flat bed was towing two.

Bryce jumped down from the first truck and looked at the other trucks. "Hey, babe." He said as he kissed my cheek. I was so confused as I read the insignia on the side of the trucks. Shadow Pack Towing. "What is this?"

"You wanted to be the pack mechanic, right?" He swept his arms to the trucks. "I brought you customers."

"I don't understand," I thought I might have a notion in my head but didn't want to jump to the wrong conclusion. Bryce swept me up in his arms and kissed me. "Arick's uncle is a tow and salvage business. They don't have a mechanic. So I worked out a contract with them to bring the vehicles here for estimates and repairs."

"Seriously?" I couldn't stop the smile from spreading across my face.

"Seriously. I'm proud you're my mate and I want you to be successful in anything you want to do." He sobered for a moment. "You're not mad, are you?"

I beamed at him. "Are you crazy? I'm over the moon!" I started bouncing toward the cars, excited as the driver's began unloading them. I got a stack of slips with some symptoms on it and I was already planning the diagnosis on each one. After the vehicles were offloaded, the trucks all backed out and left, out to go get more. "Thank you." I said, but I wanted to knock him down and take all of his clothes off and show him how grateful I was.

He cupped my face and looked down at me and I couldn't stop smiling. "Just do what you do best. You're going to be amazing at everything."

I kissed him and threw myself in his arms and wrapped my arms around his neck, holding tight to the tow slips in my hand.

And for the first time in my life, I believed in dreams coming true and that happy ever after was real.

Epilogue

Ellie

I leaned over the engine bay of one of my latest hunks of junk I was working on restoring to sell to local kids. Ricky, one of the high school boys learning this as trade, stood beside me and we were making chit chat as he changed out spark plugs and wires on the old engine.

Bryce came down the steps then, smiling at us both. I held the task light for Ricky so I couldn't really move to go see him. It was the end of the day and we were about to wrap up and Ricky would be leaving soon. Bryce came over and put his hand on my belly, now big with our baby. The baby welcomed Bryce with a kick to his hand and we both laughed.

"Can I steal her away for a bit, Ricky?" He asked.

"Sure thing. I need to be getting home anyway." Ricky nodded and walked to his car and drove off into the setting light.

"What's up?" I asked as I started closing up shop for the night.

"Arick needs to go to the city to oversee this project with the construction on the edge of town." Bryce sounded tense now.

"Okay . . . and?" I stopped what I was doing to look at him.

"That means I run the pack while he's gone." I shrugged. "Okay, that's normal." I said now, confused by why he's not telling me all of it.

"Well, it's not for a few days or a week," he said now. "It would be for a few months."

I stopped and looked at him now. "Months? What about when the baby is born?"

"We talked about it. I'll still be there, but will be acting alpha. Which means my days will be spent entirely away from you." He looked as sad as I felt. But I could accept that.

"I'm okay with it. We'll get through it like we do everything else. " I smiled and he scooped me up in his arms. "How did I get so lucky to have you, brat?" He asked. "Well, you know. Everyone is occasionally blessed with luck," I joked as he kissed down the side of my neck. "Hey, hey, hey. I've got work to do here." I pushed at his shoulders.

He took his shirt off and stepped toward me. "What? You can't get any more pregnant. I miss you so much, I want you bad." He kissed me again and I gave in, because he was right.

We had the rest of our lives to love each other and I was going to enjoy every day of it.